ROSHANI CHOKSHI

sourcebooks
casablanca

Published by Sourcebooks Casablanca, an imprint of Sourcebooks
P.O. Box 4410, Naperville, Illinois 60567-4410
(630) 961-3900
sourcebooks.com

Originally published in 2020 as an audiobook by Audible Originals.

Library of Congress Cataloging-in-Publication Data

Names: Chokshi, Roshani, author.
Title: Once more upon a time / Roshani Chokshi.
Description: Naperville, Illinois : Sourcebooks Casablanca, [2021]
Identifiers: LCCN 2021018891 (print) | LCCN 2021018892 (ebook) |
   (hardcover) | (epub)
Subjects: GSAFD: Fantasy fiction. | Love stories.
Classification: LCC PS3603.H655 O53 2021 (print) | LCC PS3603.H655
   (ebook) | DDC 813/.6--dc23
LC record available at https://lccn.loc.gov/2021018891
LC ebook record available at https://lccn.loc.gov/2021018892

Printed and bound in the United States of America.
VP 10 9 8 7 6 5 4 3 2 1

Chapter 1

Once upon a time, there lived twelve reasonably attractive princesses who, when lined up together, caused such a sight that the world agreed to call them beautiful. And so they were. Every morning when the twelve princesses were roused from sleep, their slippers appeared scuffed and worn to the sole…as if they had spent the evening dancing.

"But how could this be?" proclaimed the old king. Surely, he would've known! Surely, he would've heard the music.

Or not.

I once unleashed a bottled thunderstorm right beside his head, and he merely waved his hand before his nose and muttered, "Dear me, so sorry. Must tell the cook to leave out the beans."

And so the king devised a little plan to find out where his daughters disappeared to each night. He announced to the kingdom: "Whosoever discovers where my twelve daughters go each evening will get to choose one of them for a wife!"

You know how this part goes.

All the men showed up. There were princes and paupers, magicians, and even a magpie (the magpie claimed he was actually a prince in disguise, but no one could really confirm this). But it was the gardener's handsome young assistant who discovered the princesses' secret. (Thanks to me, of course! *I* was the one who told him, and only because I was bored and he offered to share some pie with me.) Each night they disappeared into fairyland to dance the night away, and each morning they collapsed into their beds to sleep. As his reward, the gardener's assistant chose the youngest, most beautiful princess for himself. I suppose he became a king in his own right, although who would ever entrust matters of diplomatic niceties to someone whose sole responsibility had been to spread manure on the flower beds? On second thought, perhaps that's quite fitting.

And that is where the story ends.

But that is not where *our* story ends.

You see, there were eleven other princesses.

And one of them was named Imelda.

Here is *another* once upon a time.

Once upon a time, there was an old king with three strapping sons. On his deathbed, he could not decide which of the three princes should become his heir, and so he issued a quest. Whosoever could vanquish the three dragons that had been terrorizing the king's grove of heirloom tomatoes would get the throne. The eldest brother, who was proud and strong, went to the north side of the grove and chopped off the first dragon's head. The youngest brother, who was charming and handsome, went to the south side, only to discover that the second dragon was in fact a lovely princess cursed to become a beast after she'd mocked a witch's handbag. He didn't wish to chop off her head, so instead he kissed her and won her hand.

The middle brother, who was quiet and clever, went west.

He found the last dragon and demanded to know what in the world it was doing in his father's tomato garden.

"If you must know, the tomatoes on this side of the grove have been grown from the poisoned waters of a nearby pool. I've been incinerating them so they wouldn't affect the population and local flora and fauna."

The middle brother couldn't argue with that.

He gave the dragon an official medal so that at least these incinerations would be sanctioned by the kingdom, and went back home.

The king declared the eldest brother his heir even though it didn't seem very vanquish-y to cut off the head of a particular creature who was just doing his ecological and civic duty. But that is how some things are. And so the eldest brother became a king, and although it pains me to say it, he hasn't done a half-bad job of ruling.

The youngest brother was quite content to lose out on the kingdom because now he had a fair princess, and she had her own kingdom that was conveniently lacking male heirs, and off he went.

That is where the story ends.

But that is not where *our* story ends.

You see, the middle brother's fate was quite undecided.

His name was Ambrose.

———

Nearly there, I promise.

The king from the first tale invited neighboring kingdoms from far and wide to celebrate the marriage of his daughter to the former gardener's assistant. You might recall that this daughter was one of the twelve dancing princesses. The event was host to much pomp and gossip, and although the decor was a touch gaudy and the wine was noticeably watered down, the guests thoroughly enjoyed themselves, and the whole family was equally disappointed, which is the best that can be hoped for when it comes to weddings.

It was at this celebration that Imelda and Ambrose fell in love and decided to wed.

Imelda's father, delighted that at least one of his daughters would marry a prince (one of Imelda's sisters was reportedly conversing with that dratted magpie, who may or may not even be a human, for goodness' sake), agreed to give the young couple a corner of the kingdom known as Love's Keep. It is an unoriginal yet instructive name because to protect it and for the land to grow and all the denizens within to be hale and happy, the king and queen must always be in love.

Which is perhaps why no one ever agreed to live there.

Far too much pressure.

But Imelda and Ambrose were delighted.

They wed the day after Imelda's sister's wedding breakfast (her father balked at the idea of a whole new set of expenses, and the florals were only a tad droopy) and spent a day and a night as husband and wife. But the afternoon of her own wedding brunch, Imelda fell ill after tasting the famous heirloom tomatoes from Ambrose's kingdom. The dragon had surely done its best to keep all the tainted fruit out of the crop, but tomatoes are sneaky, and this one found its way to Imelda's salad plate.

The young princess was on the brink of death. Everyone was deeply sad and shocked, especially Imelda's youngest sister, who thought it was a touch rude that someone's illness was taking attention away from *her* wedding.

But fear not, for there was a witch present. The witch, by the way, really did not look her age and had fabulous taste in handbags. She could work a powerful spell to revive the princess, but it required a price.

"I'll do anything!" Prince Ambrose declared.

Privately, the witch thought about how tedious altruism is, but publicly, she informed the prince of the cost:

"To revive her, you must give up your love for one another."

I cannot tell you what the prince's reaction was to such a decision. Did he smile? Did he look at his shoes? Did he frown?

Who knows.

All that matters is that he agreed.

———⌒———

Once upon a time, there was a king and queen in a land called Love's Keep who once loved one another, but alas, no more. Without love, they would be ousted from their kingdom at the end of a year and a day.

"What a witch takes, a witch does not give back!" their friends and family warned.

They resigned themselves to this loveless fate, knowing that at the end of it all, King Ambrose would be exiled (because that was the fashionable thing to do for ousted kings) and Queen Imelda would return to her father's kingdom and watch after her sister's brood of baby birds. (The magpie had lied after all.)

A year and a day passed.

This is where their story starts.

Chapter 2

IMELDA

Careful with those! If memory serves, that particular pair of shoes once belonged to a cannibal witch. They've got a taste for flesh. Trust me. I slipped one of them on, and the thing nearly took off my heel."

"Yes, Your Highness."

Imelda waved away the title. "I'm not sure you can even call me that anymore."

The servant paled. "I, um, my deepest apologies—"

"Don't worry," Imelda said gently. "I won't tell."

The servant blanched, then held out the box of shoes a little farther away from his person before trotting to the row of three carriages. Two of the carriages were solely for the transportation of Imelda's shoes. The other carriage was for her. As for her gowns and whatnot, they'd never really felt like they belonged to Imelda.

Each day, the magical armoire in the castle of Love's Keep grew a ball gown or a day dress, depending on her mood. The last month had been depressingly funereal—black crepe, black satin, black linen. On one occasion, the armoire had even provided a black vulture hat that squawked "ALAS!" if you ruffled its feathers. She knew how the hat felt. Imelda had given up hope almost the day she'd arrived in Love's Keep, but it was a little rude when even one's closet recognized that her situation was hopeless.

Another servant appeared at her shoulder and coughed lightly. "Queen Imelda, I—"

"I'm not a queen."

"Princess?"

Imelda muttered, "I was thinking more along the lines of 'Prisoner.'"

"Your esteemed father sent a note to be read prior to bringing you back home." The servant consulted a roll of parchment in his hands. "You are hereby required to wear shoes."

Imelda glanced at her bare feet. She dug her toes into the mud. "No."

"But, my lady, you...you have so many...surely one pair might do." The servant eyed one of the two carriages full of Imelda's heels.

"Acquiring shoes is not the same thing as deciding to walk around in them."

"But your father—"

"My father wants me to come home more than he minds the state of my dress," Imelda said grimly.

"Forgive me for asking, my lady, but why possess so many shoes if you have no wish to wear them?"

Imelda eyed the servant, then lifted one eyebrow. "I forgive you for asking."

And then she stalked off toward the carriage.

"Are you ready to go home, Queen Imelda?" the driver said brightly as he held open her door.

Imelda glanced at the carriage door, which bore her father's sigil of a beady-eyed hawk in mid-flight. *I'm always watching*, it said. *Home*, she thought. Home was supposed to mean a place of peace and rest. But she knew she would find neither of those things in her father's narrow halls. There would be only the giant room she'd once shared with her sisters, six of whom had found husbands and homes far from their father's controlling eye. Every step she took would be monitored. Every dress she wore would be decided in advance.

Home, it seemed, meant the end of freedom.

Imelda turned to the gate of Love's Keep. She'd found no love here, but she had found independence. And quiet. No screaming sisters squabbling over dresses, no younger sister sneaking into her bed because of a nightmare. No one calling her by the wrong name because "my goodness, all twelve sisters look so alike!" Enough quiet to be, well, *herself*. She danced. She painted. She read books. She helped in the village, and although she could tell her people pitied their loveless, doomed queen, they liked her anyway.

This was goodbye to all of that. Goodbye to her husband too.
Husband. What a concept.

She barely knew Ambrose, and he had made it clear early on in their days at Love's Keep that he was not at all interested in her. It was for the best. She had no wish to share her bed. She loved hoarding pillows, sprawling out sideways, and a husband would get in the way of all that.

Sometimes, she'd thought of running away, but then what? At least as queen, she answered to no one but herself. If she fled, she would always be on the run, always under the threat of being discovered and dragged back to either her husband or her father.

Perhaps it was better to know what full freedom felt like…even if it was only for a year and a day.

"It's time," said the driver firmly.

Imelda said nothing as she eased herself onto the carriage seat.

Why did *she* have to go home when Ambrose could wander out into the woods?

Imelda curled her hands into fists. "It's all just so—"

AMBROSE

"Unfair!" muttered Ambrose.

Ambrose grimaced, staring out at the dark, shadowed woods that unfurled just beyond a spit of graveled pathway that marked the boundaries of Love's Keep. He cast a longing glance at the wrought-iron gate of the castle, now closed to him forever.

He waited outside the courtyard as his elder brother, Ulrich, exited his chariot and came out to meet him. No doubt waiting to gloat as the clock struck. At noon, a year and a day would officially be up, and Ambrose would be cast out of the palace.

Ambrose hadn't slept all night. Instead, he'd walked the halls; counted the stones in the floor; ran his hand over the carved throne; dragged his finger across the edicts he'd passed, the paintings he had enjoyed pondering in a kingly manner…if even for a short while.

If there was anything his father had taught him over the years, it was that things could always be taken from you. A throne was different, though. There might be the odd challenger or furious dragon, but for the most part, a kingdom was inseparable from its king.

Ambrose felt a dull ache behind his ribs. For a year and a day, he'd had a place where he belonged, a place where he could be someone and *do* something.

For once, he was not just the lowly prince sandwiched between his kingly brothers, but a ruler in his own right, with people who looked up to him. Now he would be flung out into the wild, and all because a witch had forced him to sacrifice the one thing that would have ensured his rule.

Perhaps it would have always ended this way. A kingdom sustained on *love*? He couldn't remember the feeling, but the very idea struck him as shaky from the start. After all, love could be forever snipped out of one's heart with just a snap of a witch's fingers.

In the courtyard, a gnarled, white skeleton of a tree shot out from the stones, its dead branches twisting high enough to scrape a cloud straight out of the sky. If Love's Keep were prospering, the tree would bear jeweled fruit.

Ulrich approached him, delivered a mocking bow, and swept back his iridescent cloak.

"Little brother," he said in a poisonously sweet voice.

"I'm a king."

He'd intended to sound regal, but he suspected he'd instead sounded like a child wearing a paper crown.

Ulrich shrugged. "For what, seven more minutes?"

Ambrose narrowed his eyes. It was still seven minutes he refused to part with.

Ulrich swished about in his new cloak. "Do you like my new cloak? Dragon scales repel flames. Very handy."

"Are you afraid someone will try to set you on fire?" asked Ambrose.

"Well, *no*, but as a king, one can't be too cautious. I had another one made for dearest Octavius."

Octavius, the youngest brother, was somewhere in the southern isles, drinking out of crystal goblets and making eyes at his lovely wife. Ambrose wasn't so sure that she would appreciate her husband's cloak, considering that she'd once been a dragon herself. Albeit quite briefly.

"I would've had one made for you, but we all knew this would only last a year and a day, and these cloaks take a good six months to make."

"Your words of comfort are, as always, a balm for the soul."

"I did bring you something for your exile, though. Kings in exile must have protection from the elements as they"—Ulrich waved a hand, searching for the right phrase—"do whatever it is they do while wandering through the woods."

Languish and slowly wither into obscurity, thought Ambrose darkly.

Ulrich withdrew a small parcel wrapped in brown paper and handed it to his brother.

"I must be off now, but perhaps we'll run into each other someday in the forest. I do like hunting." Ulrich clapped him on the shoulder. "I wish you well, brother."

Alone, Ambrose stood in the empty stables and opened the parcel. It was a rough-looking, brown pilgrim's cloak. Unfortunately, he hadn't thought about a cloak, so he realized he might as well take it with him. He threw it around his shoulders and frowned.

"Dear God, what prickly creature was this thing made from anyway?"

He was about to shrug off the immensely itchy garment when the cloak tightened around his neck.

I am a horse! Observe! came a cheerful voice.

It made an attempt at neighing. But all it succeeded in doing was losing a couple of its hairs and shaking out some dust.

"You *were* a horse."

The enchanted cloak loosened around his shoulders.

I am quite certain I am a horse still, it said.

"Well, the world is certainly brimming with delusions today."

Delusions? Is that a kind of sweet?

"Why in the world would Ulrich give you to me?" Ambrose grumbled.

I believe I am to keep you from going mad.

"Splendid."

As you wander through the woods, you will always have me, your trusty steed, to talk to!

"I would rather not."

Or I can talk. I like talking.

Ambrose trudged out from the stables, watching his brother's carriage take off down a road paved with gold, enchanted to speed up travel. Too bad that the road would only answer to Ulrich. If Ambrose tried to step on it, it would vanish into dust. Still, Ambrose stared after that blinding, golden light. Why couldn't he just go to one of his brothers' palaces? Be an adviser? Scheme from the sidelines?

Why did Imelda get to go home?

Imelda. Ambrose couldn't think about her without feeling a painful twinge of guilt. She was a stranger to him, a slender shadow glimpsed from the vantage point of their shared balconies or staircases. Nothing more.

He wondered if she hated him. She must have been lonely and bored this past year. Perhaps she spent all her time mourning and missing her sisters, wishing for a husband she could love who would love her in return.

Ambrose glanced at the three carriages sent by Imelda's father. No doubt they held her jewels, dresses, trinkets, and such.

Ambrose drew himself up. Failed marriage or not, he would act like a king. And a king would bid her farewell.

He marched up the steep, grassy incline from the stables to

the waiting carriages. A breeze ruffled the silken curtains of the window, and he imagined he could see her.

And then, from deep within the carriage, came a strangled cry—

Ambrose reached for the hilt of his knife.

Something sailed out of the window at an alarming speed, smacking him right in the face.

"Ow!"

The carriage door swung open, and Imelda stepped out, brandishing a shoe and yelling:

"You can TELL my father that if he tries to put a shoe on my foot, he'll swiftly find one right up his—"

Imelda paused, seeing Ambrose.

"What are *you* doing here?" she said imperiously. "Shouldn't you be galloping through the woods on a horse?"

Ambrose stared at her, bewildered.

She asked you a question, said the cloak peevishly. Ambrose shook himself, then said:

"I don't have a horse."

False! I'm a horse! said the cloak.

Chapter 3

IMELDA

Imelda lowered her shoe, staring at Ambrose.

She couldn't remember the last time she'd seen him. A month? Two months ago? She wanted him to look ridiculous in his pilgrim outfit. But even in exile, Ambrose looked like a king.

Technically, he was a prince again, but he'd never struck her as one. Imelda had seen her share of princes. They'd all come to her father's court, hoping to marry one of the famous twelve dancing princesses. They all had this vaguely golden look about them—hair as bright as coins, eyes saucer-wide with innocence, shoulders as narrow as the worlds they'd grown up in.

Not Ambrose. He was tall and spare except for his shoulders, which looked like they ached for a heavy cape instead of that ridiculous brown cloak that believed it was a horse. If the other men's skin was as golden as syrup, his had hardened to dark amber. Golden ringlets didn't curl about his ears. Instead, he had a thick sheaf of charcoal hair held in place by a slim diadem. His eyes—the color of rocks after a rainfall—regarded her warily. There was something about his face that looked severe—a cruel set to his mouth, dark eyebrows, a sharp nose, and a sharper jaw. He would not be called handsome in the way of princes.

But he was striking.

He was also, Imelda recalled, a complete and utter stiff.

"Is there something I can help you with?"

Ambrose drew himself up. "I came to see you off."

Imelda waved her shoe and turned back to the carriage compartment. "Henceforth, please consider me *off*—"

"Aren't you forgetting something?"

She turned and saw that he had picked up her shoe.

"You can't return to court barefoot."

The word struck a nerve. Imelda narrowed her eyes. "Who are you to say what I can and cannot do?"

"Is a princess returning home without slippers supposed to be some kind of jest?"

"I am told I'm immensely funny," she said.

"It shows a complete lack of decorum. All princesses wear shoes."

"Unless such pair of slippers comes equipped with wings that bear me instead of tying me down in the muck, this *queen* shall remain without shoes."

Imelda's jaw tightened. To her, every slipper was a trap.

At home, an enchantment had been sewn into each sister's shoe so that they would do whatever the king commanded. It was to keep them safe, her father would say lovingly. It was also why the sisters slipped into the fairy world and wore out the slippers until they came apart.

Imelda watched Ambrose's scowl deepen. This was, perhaps, the longest time he'd spent in her company, and he chose to annoy her? Very well. She could do the same.

"How husbandly of you to flex your authority and such," she said coyly. "I hope you didn't wish to exercise any other husbandly duties. Or perhaps a few minutes is all you need."

Spots of color appeared on Ambrose's cheekbones.

"Someone might hear you talk like that," he said.

"Oh, do queens not know of such things? Perhaps you can instruct me on the finer points of decorum, though that might be difficult while you're wandering through the countryside with your...horse."

The cloak flipped a bit at the edges, saying, *I told you!*

Imelda turned back to the carriage, flopped onto her seat, and slammed the door shut.

"You're my *wife*," called out Ambrose, frustrated. "People will mock you, and I'm only trying to help."

Imelda poked her head through the window.

"I am not your concern. And as of today, I am *not* your wife."

She was about to knock on the carriage roof to start the horses when a flash of light burst across her eyes.

Imelda blinked, stunned to see that the door of her carriage had been thrown back and a willowy witch stood right before her.

"As usual, I have impeccable timing."

Chapter 4

AMBROSE

I f it hadn't been for the sudden appearance of the witch, Ambrose would have delivered an excellent farewell speech.

Or maybe not.

He realized with growing horror that he had no idea who he'd married. He had thought he'd wed a fair princess. But if it wasn't for that gown and tiara, she looked a bit like something that had crawled out of a forest.

And not in a bad way.

Like one of those forest nymphs, he supposed. Wild, dark hair that looked as if it were meant for catching on tree branches. Skin the color of afternoon light hitting a gold tree. Hazel eyes that made him think of a lioness.

Particularly, a lioness that looked ready to kill him.

She was pretty, but positively wild. Who would return home without *shoes*? Just the thought of all those courtier's eyes, full of ridicule, was enough to turn his stomach. He'd known those sorts of glances all his life. *"There goes Ambrose... Why can't he be more like his brothers?"*

But then the witch appeared.

He recognized her immediately. She had been at Imelda's

sister's wedding. She was the one who had stolen their love and any chance he'd had of staying king of Love's Keep. Though, given Imelda's half-wild nature, he couldn't imagine how much longer they would have lasted.

The witch was tall and slim, with a tuft of braided dandelion fluff for hair. There were apples in her cheeks and crinkles in her smile, and from the hinge of her elbow swung a ginormous satchel that looked as if it had been crafted from pink feathers.

The witch dangled her purse. "Like it?"

The hem of Ambrose's cloak swayed a bit, as if trying to catch a better look at the purse.

I've never seen a pink horse.

"It's a flamingo," said the witch.

The cloak flapped at the purse. *Hello?* The purse made no response. *What an exceptionally rude horse*, said the cloak disdainfully.

"What's the meaning of this?" Imelda demanded. "And doesn't anyone else seem to notice—"

The carriage driver was frozen mid-sprint—hand clamped on his hat, one foot kicked out before the other.

"Oh, they noticed all right," the witch said cheerily. "So I bought us some time. Two minutes should do the trick nicely."

"Trick?"

Imelda hopped down from her carriage. Excitement glowed in her eyes. It made her seem younger. Almost happy.

The witch smiled with all her teeth. "I have something to show you, something that I think might interest you. You see, I can give you that which you want most."

Ambrose went still.

The witch gestured at the pearlescent towers of Love's Keep. "If you do this errand for me, you might even get your palace back."

"Impossible," Imelda said. "We'd have to be in love."

"Who's stopping you?" asked the witch.

Ambrose and Imelda looked at one another, confused.

"*You* did," Ambrose told the witch.

"I did no such thing. Love lost doesn't have to stay that way. I can't give it back, of course, but these things have a way of growing on their own if cultivated properly. But that might not be what you wish."

Ambrose gaped. Love's Keep was the place where he had been happiest, but love was too fragile a foundation. He would not subject himself to that. Judging from the repulsed look on Imelda's face, it was clear she felt the same way.

"What do you want?" Imelda asked the witch.

"I've run out of my favorite potion, unfortunately." The witch opened her feathered purse and took out a little gray vial. "Dead useful. Turns people to statues!"

Ambrose took one step backward.

Imelda took one step forward.

"I need you to fetch me a new vial. It's not a fast job. It will take you at least a week. You see, the potion is kept on the person of a queen in a faraway kingdom. Honestly, it's not too far from here if you've got an enchanted road in your pocket"—she patted the side of her bright purse—"which I do! Sadly, this kingdom is throwing a wedding, and I tend not to be very popular at those sorts of celebrations. You see why I need you to go, don't you? You know how it is. 'All kings and queens from far and wide are invited to celebrate the nuptials of so and so.' You could easily gain entrance. Then you just have to figure out how to bring me one of those vials."

"We're no longer king and queen," Imelda said. "And I'm sure the rest of the world knows that by now."

"Let *me* handle what the rest of the world thinks they know by now, my dear. And in return, I'll give you what you want most."

"Why should we trust you?" Ambrose asked coldly.

"I figured you would ask that."

Once more, she dipped her hand into her purse. Only this time, she drew out an apple with a peel studded all over with rubies. The fruit gave off a curious fragrance, not a smell so much as an emotion. One whiff of its nectar, and Ambrose's eyes fluttered shut, his whole being filled briefly with a sense of calm. As if he were exactly where he needed to be.

Imelda gasped. "Is that…is that from—"

"That dead tree in your little courtyard? Yes."

Ambrose stared at the jeweled fruit. The tree of Love's Keep supposedly bloomed with the rare fruits only when a couple in love had taken the throne. It was said that the fruits could show you the truth of things. But it hadn't bloomed in centuries, and so there was no one to verify the tale.

"Take a bite," the witch coaxed. "See what I can promise. The fruit always speaks true, you know."

The witch pulled a paring knife out of her purse and, with two deft cuts, handed Imelda and Ambrose each one-half of the apple. Ambrose frowned at it. It could be a trap. It could be poisonous. It could be—

There was the sound of someone chomping into an apple.

Imelda had sunk her teeth into it. Her eyes fluttered shut, and a look of bliss passed over her face.

Fine, thought Ambrose. *Here goes*.

The moment he closed his eyes and bit down, magic swept through him.

He saw a kingdom of his own, the details blurry, but the feeling precise: *belonging*. An ache went through him. He felt the carved wood of a throne's armrest beneath his fingers, a warm certainty in his chest that this would not be taken from him.

His eyes flew open.

"I'll do it," Ambrose said breathlessly. "I'll find your potion and bring it to you."

With the aid of your trusty, noble steed.

"I'm coming with you," Imelda announced.

"Absolutely not."

"Absolutely *yes*."

Ambrose raised an eyebrow. "Then that will likely require you to wear shoes, which I realize you are incapable of—"

The witch cleared her throat. "I have a solution for that."

She snapped her fingers, and a stream of purple light erupted from her fingertips, poured to the ground, and snuck under Imelda's gown. Imelda lifted the hem of her dress, and the light wound its way up her ankle and then disappeared.

"That should do it, my dear. The spell will keep them clean and dry and impervious to any cuts."

"Thank you." Imelda turned to Ambrose. "Now what do you have to say?"

The cloak sighed. *I don't know where she'll find her own horse on such short notice, but I suppose I could always make room.*

"That's very generous of you," Imelda said kindly.

The cloak whickered happily.

God help me, thought Ambrose.

Chapter 5

You want to know what is truly boring?

Hearing about someone on a road.

What is there to say, really? There were a couple of birds. The sky changed. The trees darkened.

Attempts at conversation were mulled over in their skulls and quickly abandoned.

At a puddle, Ambrose—trained, of course, in courtly manners—paused and pulled off his cloak so that Imelda might step over the offending water.

Imelda stared at him, stepped around the puddle, and kept moving.

Ambrose's cloak, at least, assured him that he had done the right thing.

At another juncture in the road, there stood a man hawking wish-granting fruits and love charms, cordials of homemade brambleberry liqueur, and even some toffee apples. Imelda purchased two toffee apples and handed one to Ambrose, who took one bite, spit it out, and glared at her. Imelda was insulted. She did not pause to inspect the piece he'd thrown off to the side of the road, which bore, unfortunately, only half a worm.

The enchanted road was not the only thing the witch had given Imelda and Ambrose. There were perhaps a couple other trinkets here and there. And some granola. One can never go amiss in life with some granola. But roads are finicky. Once dusk hits, they start coiling up and languishing across the dirt, and there's no sense in trying to rile them up again until morning. Imelda and Ambrose were well aware of that fact. Besides, the witch had warned them that the journey would take more than a day, and they had no horse.

No, the cloak does not count.

Which brings us to the inn where they were obliged to stop.

Chapter 6

IMELDA

Imelda gathered up the last of the tired road in her arms.

By now, it had shrunk to the size of a voluminous skein of golden silk. At her touch, the road shivered and yawned. All at once, it zoomed back upon itself, coiling up sharp and tight so that it appeared as a palm-size spool of thread. Imelda smiled, pocketing it.

Her stomach gave a growl of hunger, but it wasn't food that she wanted... It was another bite of the witch's apple. Even now, she could taste the remnants of what it offered. That succulent, golden bite of freedom. Of *choice*. And all they had to do was bring the witch her potion.

And yet, there was something else the witch had said that troubled Imelda.

All this time, she'd thought the love lost between herself and Ambrose was gone forever, dissolved in a trade for magic. If they got it back, they could return to Love's Keep, the place that had become more of a home to her in a year and a day than all the years spent in her father's kingdom.

But she didn't want to be tied to someone.

And she couldn't imagine having ever been in love, much less falling in love *again*, with someone as stiff and pompous as Ambrose. She could tell he felt the same. She remembered the way he'd looked at her when the witch revealed the possibility of regaining what they'd lost, as if the very thought of loving her horrified him.

"This place is horrific," Ambrose said grimly.

Ambrose, she was learning, said everything grimly. He was the kind of man who seemed repeatedly offended by anything remotely disorderly. Which almost certainly included this entire village.

The end of the enchanted road had brought them to a small traveler's square hemmed in on all sides by dark, imposing trees. The dusky light only barely illuminated a jagged row of mountains behind it. In the main square stood three squat buildings. There was a farmers' market that was closed for the evening. Then a butcher's shop with the windows shuttered. And finally, a large inn filled with bright lanterns in every window and a bright-red door, where a traveling musician strummed his lute and sang to the dark.

Ambrose's dark-gray eyes swept over the village. His mouth flattened to a thin line.

"This place is certainly—"

"*Amazing!*" Imelda said cheerily. "I've never seen an inn! Or mountains! Or—"

The sound of a troubadour playing outside the inn caught her attention.

"Ah, could it be a lonesome musician?" asked Ambrose. "What a rare, exotic species."

Imelda rolled her eyes. "Believe it or not, I've never heard a traveling minstrel. My father was horrendously strict, especially about music. No fast songs, or else we'd dance. Or slow songs that would make us prone to daydreams."

Ambrose stared at her, and Imelda felt her face flush a little. She didn't mean to talk about home. But the world felt impossibly large at the moment, and she thought she could feel the cold light of stars brushing against her skin. It was glorious.

"You're smiling," noted Ambrose.

Imelda scowled at him.

"Is that a problem?"

He looked stunned. "Not at all. I've just…never seen it."

"You've never spent more than an hour in my company."

"If I'd known you were counting the minutes in my company, I might have spared more time."

There was a teasing to his voice that unnerved her. She looked at him, at his sullen mouth and arched eyebrow, the broad line of his shoulders and the imposing set to his jaw.

Imelda replied firmly, "I am glad you never bothered, for I'm certain you would've won no smiles from me."

"Careful, princess, I like challenges."

Imelda tossed her hair over her shoulder and walked to the troubadour. Her excitement quickly faded the closer they got, for the troubadour was belting out a tragic love story.

And not just any tragic love story.

Their love story.

> *"And the fair prince with his golden hair doth give their*
>   *love away!*
> *Then his lady love came back to life, and he took her for*
>   *his wife!*
> *But their love was gone forevermore, for nothing's here to*
>   *staaaay!"*

When the troubadour finished, he turned to them and grinned expectantly.

"A penny for your thoughts, me lord and lady?"

Imelda had to remember to close her mouth. She hated that this was her legacy. A terrible love song? Plus, this seemed like the kind of thing Ambrose would start a duel over because of his bizarre sense of propriety. She looked over at him…but Ambrose only looked amused.

"You got the part about the golden hair wrong," he said coolly.

Imelda's eyebrows shot up her forehead. Ambrose turned to her, his gray eyes assessing.

"Any other commentary you wish to add, my lady?"

For a moment, Imelda could only stare at him. And then she came to herself and turned toward the troubadour.

"I'll give you a golden shoe if you *never* sing that song again."

Imelda heard Ambrose's cloak rustling loudly before asking: *Does she really have a golden shoe?* Imelda grinned a little.

Ambrose looked at her, as if to say *Well? Do you?*

Obviously, thought Imelda. The witch hadn't just given them a magic road to follow. She'd also included some trinkets—a plump walnut held two pairs out of Imelda's massive shoe collection, which she insisted would come in handy at some point; three dresses; and a handful of granola, in case they became very hungry.

Imelda reached into her pocket, pulled out the walnut, snapped it open, and retrieved a golden pair of shoes, which she then handed to the slack-jawed troubadour.

"Do we have a deal?"

The troubadour gaped at the shoes, then tucked them into his jacket. He swung his lute over his shoulder and sighed.

"I wanted to be a baker anyway," he said and strolled off down the steps.

Ambrose and Imelda watched him go, then turned to one another. In his typical courtier fashion, Ambrose gestured grandly toward the door of the inn where they would have to stay for the night before getting back to the road.

"Shall we?"

Normally, the way he said it would have annoyed her to no end.

But at this moment, it didn't sound nearly as irritating.

"Thank you," she said loftily, and swept past him.

⟿

The inn was Imelda's exact idea of "warm and cozy." There was a roaring fireplace, flanked by a semicircle of rocking chairs, and niches carved into the stone where warm, flickering torches cast pools of golden light across the floor. A sign in bright calligraphy declared:

HAVE A DELICIOUS STAY!

Imelda wanted to smile at that, but she couldn't. The farther Imelda walked, the more she felt…off.

The hall was warm. The carpet was lush.

But it was strangely empty.

"If this is a traveler's inn, shouldn't it be filled with people?"

"They're sleeping. Just as we should be."

Ambrose yawned, scratching at the base of his throat. Even his delusional cloak hung from him limply, as if it had already fallen asleep.

"But what about all the jousting and drinking and slamming of dragons' heads on dining tables?"

Ambrose stared at her, and Imelda frowned.

"Surely that's what people do when they travel?"

"They don't."

"Are you sure?"

"Positive."

Imelda looked around her and crossed her arms. "I just don't think it feels right."

"Based on your extensive travel?"

Imelda stiffened. Part of her dimly recognized the jest in his voice. She understood he was teasing.

But he didn't understand where her mind flew to in that moment...all those days spent in her father's kingdom. The enchanted little chain tied around each of her sister's ankles so that even when they wandered the labyrinth of the palace grounds, they could never truly be lost. Imelda had dreamed of seeing the world, but her dreams did not fit with reality.

If Ambrose had ever taken a *moment* to understand her, he would have known that.

Ambrose stopped walking. "Imelda?" he said softly.

"Perhaps once I'm through with this quest and this sham of a marriage thoroughly dissolves, I'll have the chance to see the world."

Ambrose opened his mouth as if to respond when a door suddenly opened. Imelda whirled around, coming face to face with a red-cheeked innkeeper wearing a ring of keys from a loop on his belt.

"Hello! Might you be looking for a room this evening?"

Imelda and Ambrose responded at the same time: "Two."

Imelda looked at the innkeeper closely. What she'd thought were just apples in his cheeks now looked different in the flickering firelight. There was a ruddy sheen to his face. His eyes seemed glossy. Hungry. She recognized that expression. Each night that she had stolen into fairyland with her sisters, she'd seen the look on the faces of the fey. How they would've gobbled them up in two bites if they took the wrong step.

"I have just the one room for you and your wife—"

"Well, actually, she—"

"She *is* your wife, is she not?"

"She—"

"*She*," Imelda interrupted, "wants a second room with a second bed all to herself. Is that something *you* can offer?"

The innkeeper stared at her, a slow smile breaking across his pudgy face.

"Unfortunately not, my lady. But the room I have planned will be perfect for you both."

He turned to Ambrose and winked. "Trust me, I know just how peevish one can get when one travels with a lady love! It's all about whetting one's appetite. That'll fix you both right up."

Imelda frowned. What did *that* mean? She turned to Ambrose, who suddenly looked as if he'd been carved from stone.

The innkeeper turned away, humming to himself and fiddling with his keys.

Imelda hissed, "Tell him we'll find somewhere else!"

"Where? We'll just get through it. I'll sleep on the floor if necessary."

Ten minutes later, Imelda and Ambrose found themselves staring at a cramped bedroom with a single window that faced the woods and mountains. The walls were painted red. There were red silk scarves thrown over the three lanterns in the room. And the bed was gargantuan, covered in crimson coverlets. At its very center was a giant heart made from red rose petals. Worse...there was approximately half a foot of available floor space. They were, quite literally, trapped.

Beside her, Ambrose was busy shrugging off his horse cloak, which kept insisting that it be taken to the stables.

There's simply not enough room for a noble stallion!

Ambrose draped the cloak over a chair, then took one of the bedsheets and threw it on top. Beneath the silk, there was some indignant shuffling, but it died down after a while.

Ambrose turned to her. Without the cloak, he seemed even more broad-shouldered than usual. The ivory-colored shirt had opened a bit at the throat, and he'd rolled up his sleeves, revealing tawny forearms. His gray eyes slid to the bed, then back to her.

He sighed. "As a maiden, I'm sure you must be concerned about your honor or frightened that—"

"*Frightened?*" Imelda laughed. "Look at this atrocious dump! *That's* what's frightening."

"I'm sure the innkeeper worked very hard at putting it all together."

Imelda poked the coverlet. "He shouldn't have bothered."

She wrinkled her nose.

"Can you smell that? It's like iron. The whole bed is probably rusted all over."

"If you weren't prepared for unsavory scents, you shouldn't have come along on this quest."

"If you weren't prepared to act a smidge less than noble, we wouldn't have to be stuck in here."

"I'll take the floor."

"There is no floor, and I might end up stepping on you when I wake up. You made your bed. Now you have to sleep in it."

Ambrose leaned against the wall. "Sleep in it? With...*you?*"

"No. With the innkeeper. Of course me!"

"We're not married," he said.

"Debatable."

"I wouldn't call a day and a night a real marriage. I don't even know if we ever..."

"We could have," Imelda mused. She paused. "We just may not remember."

They fell silent. It was a thought that had crossed Imelda's mind more than once. Surely, they must've...at some point... right? They'd been married for a day and a night before that cursed tomato had gotten to her and everything had changed.

Imelda stared at the bed, some nameless feeling snaking through her. She hadn't shared a bed in a year and a day, and she'd gotten used to sprawling out on the silks. The sound of her own breath. It was perfectly fine. But that didn't mean she hadn't imagined different scenarios.

At night, when her thoughts grew untamed, she wrapped her arms about herself and pretended they belonged to someone else. She wondered what it would be like to spend the night in a bed and never once sleep.

Her eyes darted to Ambrose. He was watching her intently. A moment later, he tore his eyes away, shaking his head.

"I'll go talk to the innkeeper," he said gruffly.

Imelda grabbed his arm. "I think *not*. I don't trust that creepy man."

"He's not creepy."

Imelda leveled him with a look.

"Okay, he's a little creepy. But I really think—"

Imelda pushed his chest, and he fell back on the bed. He sat there for a long moment, propped up on his elbows, his eyes wide. It looked more than a little strange to see him sprawled out like that. His legs were long and kicked out in front of him. His hair—usually held back by a circlet—had fallen over his forehead. An almost amused smile touched his lips. He looked at Imelda, storm-gray eyes pinning hers, before he raised an eyebrow.

The sight of him unnerved her, and so she spoke quickly:

"See? It hasn't killed you."

"And yet—"

But Imelda never heard the end of the sentence. Just then, the bed rattled to life. The coverlets arced upward in a crimson wave, trapping Ambrose against the mattress. The four iron posts snapped above him, caging him within. And suddenly, the idea of sharing a bed together struck Imelda as very deadly indeed.

Chapter 7

AMBROSE

*A*nd this, thought Ambrose, *was why one mustn't share a bed with a woman one was not exactly married to.*

One moment you could be looking at her, on the verge of an excellent witticism…

The next you would find yourself attacked by a feral mattress.

Too late, he saw the signs that must have been apparent to Imelda. The lack of strangers in the inn. The sign that suggested HAVE A DELICIOUS STAY. Ambrose couldn't decide what he hated more: that a bed was about to kill him or that Imelda was right.

"Get! The! Hell! Off! Me!" Ambrose shouted.

Ambrose saw that the red sheets had tangled their way around his leg, and now his torso. A pillow kept batting at his face. In his right pant leg, there was a small knife. Ambrose tried to inch his way toward the blade—

The bed tensed.

It knew.

The mattress folded sharply inward, and Ambrose gasped for air. This was it. He was going to die. Trapped in a bed that was quite possibly trying to eat him and without having done anything remotely exciting within it.

Heat flashed over his face. He squinted against the sudden brightness slicing through the red fabric. The bed gave off a metallic shriek, its iron hinges squealing suddenly as the silks drew back from his chest. Not enough room to see, but enough room to frantically gulp down air.

Finally, he could reach down his pant leg, pulling at the small knife tucked around his calf.

One cut, then two—

The silk sheets gave way to...*fire*.

Flames rippled across his sight, and he startled backward. The fire jerked away from his face, and now Ambrose could see that it belonged to a torch held aloft in Imelda's hand.

"It was the only thing I could think of!" Imelda yelled. "Get out!"

The bed squealed and howled. Imelda lowered the flame to the pillow.

"That's for being gaudy!"

Ambrose threw off the last of the coverlets, then rolled onto the floor, where he ran smack dab into the wall. He flung his hand upward, grasping the latch of a small window that overlooked a ten-foot jump to the ground. From the staircase came the sound of heavy footfalls and the delighted chortling of the innkeeper, followed by the hushed mutterings of a small crowd.

"What if the bed hasn't ate 'em up yet?" someone said.

Imelda inched toward the door, holding the torch aloft.

Ambrose shook his head vigorously as he reached to unclasp the latch of the window. Imelda ignored him.

Now the innkeeper spoke. "Nah, the bed always finishes them off right quick—"

Ambrose shuddered at that, sneaking a glance at the giant crimson bed. Now it cowered toward one end of the room, as if trying to keep a wide berth from Imelda and her flaming torch. With a jiggle and a jerk, Ambrose got the window to swing open noiselessly.

He reached for his sword belt and the horse cloak. The cloak snorted awake.

"I need you to be a rope!"

But I'm a horse.

"I need you to be a horse rope."

I don't think that is a thing.

Ambrose ignored the cloak, hanging it off the side and gesturing wildly at Imelda.

But she refused to move as more voices gathered outside the door.

"But did *he* finish off right quick? Meat's always tastier when it's had a bit uh tendering, if you know what I mean."

"That hellion of a wife could do with some tendering—"

"She'd be awful in a cake."

"A slow boil maybe…like a stew."

"Shrew stew!"

Then they were chanting: "Shrew stew! Shrew stew!"

Imelda looked about, ready to bash their heads in with the torch.

"Come on!" Ambrose whispered loudly.

But Imelda wasn't looking at him. She was muttering "shrew stew" under her breath and adjusting her grip on the torch.

The door flung open, and the innkeeper and his crew of cannibals trundled inside. They took one look at the crimson bed, huddled in a corner, and had approximately two seconds to frown before Imelda swung back her torch and caught the innkeeper right in his teeth.

Imelda was alarmingly proficient with a torch in her hand. She spun it, sweeping someone's feet out from under them. Then she rammed the butt of the torch into the stomach of another, who fell with a grunt. In a few moments, she'd made quick work of them, and when she turned to Ambrose, there was a vicious grin on her face.

"How's that for tender?" Imelda spat breathlessly.

Ambrose realized that he was rather limply holding his sword in his hand.

"Not bad."

Imelda's grin widened, but it was cut short by the sound of more footsteps on the stairs. The din of voices grew louder.

And angrier.

Ambrose grabbed her arm. "Time to go!"

"But—"

"That torch took them by surprise, but they'll be conscious soon."

Ambrose climbed out the window, tugging once to make sure the horse cloak was secure.

That was my tail!

"What are you doing?" Imelda demanded.

"Escaping." Ambrose tugged the knotted cloak again just to be sure, then he looked up at her. "With you."

Imelda crossed her arms. "I am *not* jumping out a window—"

Behind her, the door swung open.

"You're quite right, princess." Ambrose wrapped his arm around her waist, pulling her close. "*We* are jumping out a window."

"Wait!"

Ambrose wrapped his free hand around the horse cloak, then leapt. Cold air hit his face. Imelda turned hers to his chest. Her dark hair nearly blinding him, he held her tight. Maybe it was the fall, that weightless lurch in his stomach, that heightened every other sensation. For one brief moment, he was painfully aware of Imelda's body clasped against his own. Her leg wrapped around his, the satin of her dress clinging to the lush contours of her body. And the scent of her…

Imelda smelled like smoke.

Like the aftermath of a lightning strike. And just beneath that scent, something faintly sweet. Like burnt sugar beneath a dollop of cream.

It was utterly jarring.

But not nearly as jarring as the moment when they hit the ground with an unceremonious *thud*.

Ambrose tucked her under his arm, rolling them across the grass to break their fall. The moment they stopped, Imelda scrambled out of his grasp, breathless and wild-eyed.

Beneath him, his horse cloak stirred limply.

That hurt.

Ambrose threw the cloak over his shoulder.

Someone leaned out the window far above them, pointing and shouting.

"They're getting away! To the courtyards! Go!"

Ambrose forced himself to stand. Just beyond Imelda loomed the dark line of trees, their branches shining like knife blades in the moonlight. He darted forward, catching Imelda's hand as, together, they ran deep into the woods.

⁓

A few hours later, Ambrose tossed the last of the branches onto the fire. The sap crackled and popped, throwing sparks into the air. Imelda sat before it, warming her hands. The horse cloak was wrapped snugly around her shoulders, neighing softly in its sleep.

Behind her was the makeshift tent Ambrose had constructed,

strung together with the enchanted dresses that Imelda had pulled out of a walnut. Sapphire and silver silk billowed gently in the woods. Up here, the mountainous air was crisp but not frigid, and the thick line of trees kept them safe and out of sight.

Ambrose sat down on the log beside Imelda.

She hadn't said much since they'd run into the woods. He thought she would be furious or scared, but that arch smile hadn't left her face since she'd knocked out the innkeeper with a torch.

"That was rather fun," she said.

"*Fun?*" he said in disbelief. "You almost killed me."

"I saved your life," she said primly.

"Just barely. You couldn't wait for me to get out of the sheets before you set them on fire?"

"Isn't that the opposite of what most men want?"

Ambrose stared at her, and then, because he couldn't help himself, he laughed. Imelda grinned at him. For a few long minutes, they settled into a warm silence, and a disconcerting daydream hit Ambrose: Was this what it would have been like between them?

"You know, you're quite strange," she said.

And just like that, the daydream fell apart.

"No need to flatter me."

"It's a compliment in its own way. Since when does a noble prince who is severely concerned with whether or not one is wearing shoes know how to pitch tents in the middle of the woods? Or build fires from nothing? Wouldn't you be…I don't know… sitting by your host's fire and strumming a lute or something?"

Ambrose sighed.

"Perhaps said noble princes got locked out of their rooms quite often as punishment. And so they had to learn to make their own fires. Or sing lullabies to fall asleep. And keep warm when it grew cold."

He wasn't sure what made him tell the truth in that moment. Perhaps it was because he'd almost gotten eaten by a bed. Or perhaps because out here, the stars in the sky seemed closer, as if this moment was cut off from the rest of the world.

Imelda watched him with those strange lioness eyes. Then she drew her knees to her chest, staring into the flames.

"I would've loved to spend a whole night under the stars. My father would never let me or my sisters do that. He was rather controlling."

"You?" Ambrose said in disbelief. "Controlled?"

He was beginning to think Imelda could not be commanded to do anything other than what she wished.

"Well, it's easy to be controlled when you and your sisters all have matching enchanted shoes." Imelda wiggled her bare toes at the fire.

Understanding clicked through his thoughts, and shame warmed his cheeks.

"What did he want?" he asked gently.

Imelda met his gaze over the flames, and he felt momentarily stunned to silence as he watched the firelight limn her hair and turn her eyes incandescent.

"To protect us. He loved us, you know. He just had a strange way of expressing it. I think he thought that if we looked and acted alike, someone wouldn't be able to choose which of us to harm, and would thus leave us alone."

Ambrose let out a low laugh. "You know, I think my father wanted the same for me and my brothers, not so he could protect us, but rather so he'd have a matched set of perfect sons. I always managed to disappoint. My brother could cut off the head of a dragon with ease, but I ended up giving one a paid-benefits position in the castle. My other brother could charm sirens to sleep, but if

I sang, a giant kraken would mistake me for her long-lost son, and I'd be stuck grappling with it for ages and somehow emerge with a new trading contract over the seas."

Imelda laughed. "Really?"

"Oh yes. My father was...well, let us say that he was not pleased."

"Why not? Sounds like you just made things better for your kingdom, not worse."

Ambrose would've liked to think the same thing. But that was not how his father saw it.

"I suppose it's simply not how things are done."

His father wanted all his sons to be powerful, and to that end, his only lesson was that anything given could be taken away, and one must have the will and power to right the situation.

For a good deed, he would sit at his father's right-hand side. For a bad one, he'd take his meal in the kitchens. Once, he was rewarded with a puppy. Then he was punished and had it taken away.

His father had taught him distance.

If he could want so little, then very little could hurt him. If he learned early that everything could be taken away, then he would be attached to nothing but the pursuit of power.

When Ambrose was a child, he'd actually dreamt of something so powerful it could never be ripped from him. Years ago, he'd thought perhaps it might be true love, the kind sung about in court-yards or scribbled about in poems. But all he had to do was get married to discover how that, too, could be snatched away as easily as a handful of coins.

Things could always be taken from you.

Ambrose turned his head to the night sky, quietly willing the dawn to come faster. He didn't like being left alone with Imelda. It disquieted him, and he'd hardly been with her for more than a day.

"So your father would leave you outside the castle, and mine wouldn't let me out," Imelda remarked thoughtfully.

"We sound rather pitiful."

"We sound *alive*. That bed would've eaten us."

"Well, then, here's to us."

They didn't have anything for a cup, so they used Imelda's utterly pristine pair of crystal shoes.

"To having what we want," Imelda said.

"To unenchanted shoes," Ambrose added.

"And dragons that pose no moral conundrums."

Ambrose smiled. "And siblings we can be as similar or dissimilar to as we like."

"And to never, *ever* sharing a bed together again." Imelda shuddered.

Ambrose grinned, clinking his shoe to hers. But as he did so, he felt a twinge of awareness that he couldn't push aside. He didn't want to remember how she'd felt in his arms when they'd skimmed down the wall of the inn. How she'd smelled of smoke and burnt sugar. Or how, right now, the firelight edged her unruly curls and painted her skin gold. Perhaps it was a blessing that he didn't remember what it was like to love her. Emotion was a dangerous temptation, one that only brought loss.

"Never again," he said.

And then he drained his glass.

—⊷—

As you know by now, roads are exceptionally boring. No one wants to hear about them, least of all me, and I love the sound of my own voice.

What isn't boring, however, are woods.

Everyone loves a good tale where some clever fox or kindly

grandmother steps out of the woods, bearing advice and goodwill and what have you. Want to know why? It's because people are lazy! I can't tell you how many youngest sons I run into in the woods on a daily basis.

"Dear witch," they say. "Won't you help me, and I shall part with the meal my father packed?"

PAH!

Do some research! Invest in a map! Don't just lollygag about, waiting for some hungry, wise woman to stumble upon you. And don't count yourself lucky when I do stumble upon you, boy.

"Oh, aren't you sweet," I usually end up saying, stroking their cheeks.

And you know, with a good bottle of port, some aged cheese, and my finest cherry jam…they are, in fact, rather sweet.

Chapter 8

IMELDA

The next morning, Imelda pushed open the makeshift curtains of her tent and found Ambrose passed out on a log.

His dark hair fell over his forehead. One arm was propped beneath his head. She noticed that he frowned while he slept, and that he had long eyelashes that lightly fanned over his cheekbones. It struck her like a wave how little she actually knew him. He'd always moved through Love's Keep like an imposing shadow. She didn't imagine he could laugh the way he had. Or that the sound of it—like joyful thunder—would be something she wanted to hear again, knowing that her jesting words had been the cause of it. She hadn't imagined, either, how it felt to be *held* by him, even if it was only because they'd needed to jump out a window. She'd felt the hardness of his chest, the heat of his hands on her waist…

And she didn't mind it.

If her life had gone as planned, would this be what she would have woken up to every day?

Normally, she would've balked at the thought of something so staid and routine, but she felt no disgust. Just a strange pang of curiosity…one that would have to remain a curiosity. Yesterday had only proven to her that she would never survive in the confines of a castle. She wanted a life ripe with adventure, where she answered to no one and nothing.

That would never happen if she fell in love.

Imelda took a step backward, only for a branch to snap underfoot.

Ambrose stirred awake. He blinked, staring up at her before scrambling to his feet.

"Imelda?" he said groggily.

His voice was deeper. Rougher. She could feel it resonating in her bones.

"Who else did you expect? I take it you are not a morning person," she said.

His gaze flitted over her face.

Imelda stiffened. Could he tell somehow that she'd been watching him sleep? She immediately turned before he could examine her any further. In a few swift motions, she'd taken the dresses down from the tent. Next, she pinched the fabric between her thumb and forefinger, and the garments instantly shrank until they were small enough to fit inside the walnut shell that the witch had given her.

"We should get back to the road," Ambrose said.

The horse cloak wiggled its hem, as if kicking hooves in its sleep, and murmured, *I don't want to gallop.*

"Wouldn't the woods be safer? Those cannibals might still be looking for us. There has to be another road leading out of it."

"If we go into the woods, we don't know what we'll find. It could be full of beasts or something terrible. We should stick with the plan we were given."

"How innovative," Imelda said dryly. "And how did that decision to work with the plan we were given go over at the inn?"

Ambrose opened his mouth. Closed it.

"Fine," he said tightly. "Just follow my lead, do what I say, and we'll be safe."

Imelda scowled. *Follow my lead?* As if she hadn't proven last night that she was perfectly capable of defending herself, saving him, and even detecting when there was trouble on the horizon? If he had just trusted her the moment she said that the innkeeper struck her as creepy, they wouldn't even be in this state.

"As you command, my king," she muttered.

⸺᠂

Gleaming sunshine sifted through the trees, and pollen spangled the air like golden dust. Birds the color of gemstones alighted on sunlit branches, and the world seemed drenched with wonder and possibility.

But one wouldn't know that the way Ambrose acted.

Every time they crossed over a tree's shadow, he looked likely to jump.

"Careful," he said. "There might be bears."

"If there *are* bears, I highly doubt you standing half a foot away from me solves anything."

"I'm trying to protect you. The last thing we want is one of those beasts chasing after us. If that happens, how, exactly, would I keep you safe?"

"One, that really isn't your responsibility," Imelda said, annoyed. "And *two*, if you're truly that concerned, then simply don't run as fast as me. We don't have to outrun a bear, you know. One of us just has to present it with a more easily accessible supper."

"Very funny, Imelda."

Though the woods were far from treacherous, there was still no sign of another road.

And if they didn't find it, they'd fail the witch's task, and Imelda would end up right where she started: trapped in her father's kingdom.

Imelda threw up her hands. "Maybe we should just turn back around, take our chances with the cannibals—"

"Are you looking for a road?" an unfamiliar voice cut in.

IT'S A BEAR! the horse cloak squealed.

A wide shadow seeped out from the space between two trees. There was the sound of crunching leaves and branches broken underfoot. Ambrose moved closer to her, holding his sword aloft. Imelda desperately wished she had a weapon, but she didn't, and it was now far too late to reach for an extra heel tucked into that walnut bag.

"You looking for a road?"

Imelda's heartbeat ratcheted up as something stepped out from between the creatures. Not a person at all, but a long…lean…

"Skunk?" she ventured aloud.

The creature glared. It was about knee-height, standing on its back paws, and the color of charcoal, with a bright-pink nose and a strip of white fur that ran down its back and tail.

"Honey badger, actually. The name's Charming."

"Seems like a name more suited to a prince than a badger," Imelda observed.

Charming grinned, and Imelda noticed that the creature's teeth were needle sharp.

"What a unique joke. So, uh, listen. I hear you're lookin' for a road."

"No we're not," Ambrose said quickly.

"*Yes* we are," Imelda said.

Ambrose threw Imelda a warning look.

"I can help you with that."

"We don't need your help, thank you," said Ambrose.

"What, just because Imma honey badger?" Charming thumped his chest. "You gotta problem with that, big man?"

"We don't want any trouble, we just need to get going. Thank you for your kind offer. Goodbye."

Ambrose started to walk away, but Imelda held her ground.

"Excuse me. Would you give us a moment?"

The badger rolled its eyes. "Sure, why not. Is this what passes for common decency around humans these days? I might as well just forgeddaboutit."

Imelda tugged on Ambrose's sleeve, drawing him into the shadow of a nearby elm.

"What are you doing?" she asked, scowling. "He could help us!"

"He's a badger."

A honey badger, the horse cloak corrected him.

Ambrose shrugged off his cloak and bundled it under his arm, despite its loud protestations.

"So why does that mean he can't help us?" Imelda asked.

"It doesn't. But I know how these talking-animal types get. They say they'll help you, but they always want something in return—"

"I don't think reciprocity is that damning."

"Sure, but what they want can be ridiculous. Like, go get them a castle. Or find a dragon egg or something like that."

"You're being ridiculous. What if he wants some food? Or he's just being nice?"

"Now *you're* being ridiculous. Everything has a cost, Imelda. *Everything.* Just do as I say and we'll get out of this."

Well, that does it, thought Imelda.

"Honey badger!" she called loudly. "What do you want in return for showing us the way to the road?"

Charming scuttled a little closer, tenting his paws.

"Well, I wasn't about to ask for anything, you see. But now that you, uh, mention it…"

Imelda's stomach sank a bit. In the same second, Ambrose shot her a look that defiantly stated *I told you so*.

"I'm really hungry," Charming said pathetically. "It's hard to get food around here… I was hoping you could just get an apple for me? I know a tree not too far off. If it's not too much trouble, you see."

Now Imelda turned triumphantly to Ambrose.

"It's no trouble at all."

———❧———

The badger led them to a courtyard hidden deep in a thicket of trees. A circle of stones veined all over with moss stood in the ruins of an ancient palace. Just beyond the courtyard stood a copse of autumn-gold trees. Perhaps once it had been a royal orchard, but now it grew utterly wild in the absence of humans.

Imelda spread her arms wide and inhaled deeply.

There was the scent of fallen pears in the air—round and sweet. Dusky plums the color of nighttime peered at them through the branches. The apple tree was far off and framed by a high, unbroken wall of stones. Even from here, Imelda could see that the branches were thick with golden fruit. Their peel was pockmarked from birds, and yet when the wind brushed past them, Imelda imagined that she could hear them softly chime.

Charming rose up on his hind legs, rubbing his paws mournfully. "One, uh, them, please."

Seemed easy enough.

But Ambrose frowned. "Why *that* tree?"

Imelda elbowed him in the ribs.

Charming looked abashed. "It's not for me. It's for my wife, you see. She's been having some serious cravings for that golden apple. I gotta bring it back to her. Will you help me or not?"

Ambrose's eyes narrowed. "What about the road?"

"It's just past the orchard, down the hill. I promise! Would I lie to you?"

He smiled, revealing his needle teeth.

I don't like him, whispered the horse cloak.

Imelda rolled her eyes.

"For goodness' sake, I'll go and get it."

Charming darted in front of her.

"My lady! I couldn't possibly ask you to do such a thing. What with your fair princess complexion and all that. Besides, you vouched for me! I would've taken you to the road no matter what. But I gotta sense of honor, ya know? I can't take that clown to the same road unless he does something for me. It's just simply reciprocity. Quid pro quo, you know how it is."

Imelda turned back to Ambrose, and he met her gaze stonily.

"Fine. Come with me, beast."

Imelda looked around the beautiful ruins of the palace, wanting to make her way slowly, but there was no time. Biting back a sigh, she made as if to go with them, when Charming shook his head.

"There's no need for that, fair princess."

Imelda opened her mouth to correct him that she wasn't

actually a princess, but she didn't feel like explaining the whole thing right now. The moment they left, she took to climbing over the ruins, plucking plums, and tracing the letters etched into stone. Alone, she perched atop a boulder and touched her ankle… It was bare. Free of any silver chain.

She could run if she wanted…

So she did.

And it was only when she returned, breathless and grinning, that she saw Ambrose making his way back to her from the orchard. Imelda paused, waiting for her breath to slow down in her lungs.

Ambrose walked toward her with that same regal purpose that made him look like a king no matter what he wore. The sunlight caught on his dark hair, and his gray eyes snapped to hers. Imelda felt something leap deep inside her chest.

Ambrose moved closer. Now he was less than five feet away, and yet he still hadn't said anything to her. When she looked at him, a sly grin curved his mouth. It made him look handsome, but somewhat cruel. It didn't suit him.

"What happened to Charming?"

"Forgettaboutit."

Only then did she notice that his horse cloak was gone too.

"You left your cloak behind! You know how sensitive it gets—"

Ambrose moved closer. Something around his neck caught the light. A strange amulet that she could've sworn he hadn't been wearing earlier. *His voice*, thought Imelda. *It sounded different.*

"Are you well?" she asked.

He smiled with all his teeth. He was standing close. Close enough that she could count his eyelashes. Her pulse stammered a bit when his eyes lowered to her lips.

"I will be."

His hand slipped quickly behind her neck, dragging her to him as he kissed her hard on the mouth.

Chapter 9

AMBROSE

A mbrose had never been brought so low in his life.

Literally.

The thought kept occurring to him as he scampered across the forest floor, his new black-furred belly beneath him.

One moment, he had been standing in the orchard, plucking an apple for that sharp-toothed Charming, who kept rubbing his paws together. The next moment, he had found himself bowled over, a piece of golden fruit shoved behind his teeth while Charming clamped his jaws together and forced him to swallow. Charming had stamped his clawed foot on a vaguely depressed piece of dirt, and traps had sprung up around Ambrose's arms and legs, clamping him into place.

Charming shouted triumphantly, "That's it! There's the ticket! Just one little bite, and I'll be you and you'll be me and everything will be such glee!"

Ambrose struggled against him, but Charming was almost preternaturally strong. Flung off from his arm, his horse cloak struggled to move closer, declaring:

Have a care for my master!

"Oh, no." Charming laughed. "Honey Badger don't care *at all*! I've been stuck in this miserable form for too long!"

I'll—I'll fight you! the horse cloak declared.

Ambrose's lungs strained. He had no choice. He swallowed the fruit whole.

Heat wound down from his throat and spread through his ribs. His hands seized up, fingers curling tightly toward his palm. Ambrose started to thrash wildly. In front of him, Charming started to grow and transform. His narrow snout pulled downward, his black eyes took on a gray hue, and thick spurts of dark hair tufted out from his ears.

"Yes!" Charming yelled. "YES! Finally!"

Light burst around him. Ambrose was free. Free in the sense that he was no longer restricted by the traps.

"Sorry about all that, pal." Charming-Turned-Ambrose straightened his sleeves. "You know how it is. And I'm sorry about this next part, too, but I really can't have you trying to reverse the spell on me. It's gotta hold until I kiss my fair bride."

Charming winked at him with Ambrose's eye. Gold glinted about his neck, and Ambrose realized he was wearing a necklace with a heavy pendant shaped like an apple.

Charming snapped his now-human fingers, and a trail of flame burst up around the apple tree.

"See ya!" Charming strolled forward without a backward glance.

The flames gathered, swirling around Ambrose and trapping him on all sides. As a badger, his pulse felt erratically quick, as if he were being hunted. He scuttled backward, paws skidding on the slick leaves beneath him. And then—

There was a swooshing sound as the horse cloak came to the rescue.

I've got you, master!

The horse cloak squirmed and writhed on top of him, and

smoke filled Ambrose's lungs as the cloak's sudden embrace snuffed out the fire. Ambrose rolled away, now neatly sidestepping the traps that Charming had set. He coughed, gasping for air.

"Thank you," he said.

But it came out as a high-pitched squeak.

It didn't seem to make a difference to the horse cloak, though, for its hem gathered like a loop and then folded down, like a head bent in acknowledgment.

As a trusty steed, I am always by your side.

"We have to get back to Imelda!"

Most assuredly! Hop up on my back!

"Um—"

The horse cloak dove beneath him, and Ambrose-the-Badger fell onto his back as they careened through the woods.

On the one hand, being turned into a creature was a bit of a revelation. He had no idea how many smells actually existed in the world, but his finely honed badger senses meant that he could parse out everything. He could taste the sunlight spreading across a fallen leaf, hear the exhale of an uncurling root deep beneath him, and even see a dewdrop clinging to an apple blossom in all its glorious, prismatic detail.

All of which meant there was no way in the world that he could miss Imelda screeching on the other side of the orchard.

Ambrose and the horse cloak had zoomed back toward the ruined courtyard just in time to see Imelda kissing him. Wait. No. Kissing *Charming*. For a moment, the visual was just too…strange. Is that what it would look like to kiss her? Would her eyes flutter shut like that? Why did that *badger* get to wear his form and suddenly know what it felt like to sink his fingers through her hair? Heat clenched in his belly.

Ambrose growled.

"I think the *hell* not."

Unfortunately, in badger form, it just sounded like more squeaking.

⚬⚬⚬

Imelda shoved Charming-Turned-Ambrose away. "What the hell do you think you're doing?"

Charming patted his shirtsleeves and plucked at his pants.

He muttered to himself. "Huh, this ain't working quite like I imagined. But I did all the right stuff. I ate the fruit. I made the guy eat the fruit. I've kissed the princess. What am I getting wrong here?"

Imelda slapped him (well, not *him* but certainly his face), and Charming winced out of instinct. "Are you out of your mind, Ambrose?"

"I'm simply, er, caught by my affection. Overwhelmed by my sudden infatuation for you all over again, my darling—"

Ambrose-the-Badger scraped his back paws across the horse cloak and then squeaked out:

"CHARGE!"

The horse cloak sailed into the air, and Ambrose leapt off, catching onto Charming's belt loops with his sharp nails and scuttling up his body. Imelda screamed. Charming flung him off. Ambrose felt a terrible weightlessness gripping his stomach as he soared over a plum tree and crashed against a half-broken rock wall.

Imelda stumbled backward.

"Shall we, my love?" said Charming in an oily voice. "It doesn't do for husbands and wives to fight. Let's forget all about this mess."

Ambrose-the-Badger stirred weakly from his position by the rock wall. Even his near-perfect creature vision felt stilted and sluggish. And yet his eyes clapped on the glinting golden chain around Charming's neck.

He tried to take a step forward, but the whole world seemed to bleed out around the edges. His body hurt, and his tail hung limply at his side. He lifted his head. Imelda loomed over him like a giantess.

"Ambrose?"

This close, her voice sounded like a thousand gongs ringing in his ear.

"Yes, it's me!"

More irate squeaks ensued.

"That apple he ate cured him of his need for human speech, my darling wife. Pay no mind to him, and let's be on our way back home."

Imelda froze. She fixed Ambrose-the-Badger with a hard stare. He couldn't be sure what she meant by that glance. Imelda turned back around slowly.

At her feet, the horse cloak tried to roll around her ankles, as if nagging eagerly for her attention.

"Husband, is it?"

She stooped, reaching for a cluster of wildflowers that grew not too far from her feet.

"Yes, dear?" Charming said triumphantly.

Imelda's fingers brushed over the crumpled horse cloak. Charming stilled. At the same moment, Ambrose willed himself to a stand.

"I don't have a husband."

Imelda seized the horse cloak and threw it over Charming.

No matter how much Charming thrashed, the horse cloak clung to him. Charming let out a howl.

"This! Is! Not! How! This! Is! Supposed! To! Go!"

"It's not? Do inform me," said Imelda blithely.

Ambrose, who kept winking in and out of consciousness, only caught the muffled offerings of "the witch's promise" and "a human prince" and "kissing a true princess" before Charming managed to throw off the horse cloak. Imelda grabbed hold of him by the neck, then reached for the golden necklace at his throat.

"No! Not that!" Charming wailed. "Without it I'll—"

There was a snap as Imelda tore off the necklace. Golden light spread across the courtyard. Ambrose's skull suddenly felt as though someone had managed to fit a thunderstorm inside it. He blinked a couple of times, and the world swam in and out of focus—colors lost their depth, distant sounds dissolved from his consciousness, and the things that were once huge appeared small. His pulse slowed, no longer creature frantic, but thudding powerfully through his body.

He looked down at his paws…

And realized they were hands.

He was human once more, with his clothes magically restored to his body, though slightly more torn up than they had been earlier. He winced, gingerly touching the swelling knot at the back of his head. He felt as if he'd drained an entire tankard of beer.

Ambrose looked up and saw Imelda holding a golden chain in her hand. On the ground before her, Charming scuttled backward, fully a badger once more. Before he could scamper off, Imelda reached into her pocket, drawing out a sharp-heeled shoe. She flung it to the ground, neatly trapping his foot to the forest floor. Charming yelped.

"This, uh…this don't look too great for me, does it?"

"No," Imelda said flatly. "It looks as if you took advantage of my kindness, tricked us, stole Ambrose's body, stole a *kiss* from me, and proved that you're every bit the weasel you look like."

"Honey badger, actually—"

Imelda turned to the horse cloak. "Watch him, will you?"

The cloak flopped forward as if it were galloping, then fanned out its fabric around the badger, batting him every time he tried to squirm loose. Imelda turned on her heel, marching toward Ambrose.

"Are you all right?" she asked.

"Considering I was briefly a rodent, not particularly."

"Carnivorous mammal," Charming muttered.

The horse cloak smacked Charming with the edge of its hem.

Ambrose forced himself to stand, then reached for his sword.

"Oh no, wait a minute." Charming raised his paws. "I wasn't lying about the road! It's right behind the hill! Trust me!"

Imelda scowled. "Poor choice of words."

"Ah, c'mon, lady, you can't blame me for trying! I was a magician, you know. Very handsome, too, or so I recall, and then I got cursed for no reason."

The horse cloak raised its hem threateningly.

"Okay, fine, maybe I was courting a witch and didn't let her know there was another witch I was sending letters to in a different country… But I never said we were exclusive…"

Another smack from the horse cloak.

Charming went on angrily, "My *point* is I don't get my human form back unless I convince a man to eat from the Tree of Transformation and then kiss a princess! It should've worked. I don't know what I did wrong."

Imelda stepped forward, and Charming flinched.

"I'm not a princess. I'm a *queen*."

Then she gathered the horse cloak, flinging it over her shoulder as if it were an ornate shawl.

"Let's go."

Ambrose's eyebrows shot up his forehead. He couldn't stop the smile spreading slowly across his face. He fell into step beside her.

"If the lady insists."

As they headed for the hills, Charming called out to them, "If there's no hard feelings, would you mind taking a survey? Was it the honey badger form that you found most alluring? I was thinking about trying to turn myself into a fox for the next passersby. Or should I just skip all this and pretend I'm the cursed prince of this palatial dump and hope it all works out?"

Ambrose and Imelda ignored him.

"Hellooo? Could I at least get freed from the *shoe*?"

—⁂—

Charming, as it turned out, might have been a terrible badger... but he was right about the road. It emerged suddenly from the line of trees, stretching out like an unbroken line of gold. Its sudden emergence caught Ambrose by surprise because all this time, he hadn't taken his eyes off Imelda.

The light clung to her differently now.

It wasn't just her eyes that now reminded him of a lioness. It was all of her. The tangled mane of her hair, the wild and regal grace of her walk. He couldn't stop looking at her. Part of him wanted to smack himself. He'd had a year and a day to know her... to look at her...and he'd wasted every second of it.

The other part of him was grateful he'd never bothered.

Imelda was becoming more dangerously fascinating by the minute, and something inside him flinched at the realization.

His eyes fell to the forest floor. With every step, he saw a flash of her bare feet, and shame coiled in his gut.

She'd spent her life under someone else's thumb, and he'd had the nerve to command her.

She was no one's to command.

Ambrose knew he was many things. Too serious, too stoic, too proud.

But he always knew when he was wrong.

"Imelda, I—"

"I'm sorry," she cut in, breathlessly. "Though it absolutely pains me to say it, you were right about the beaver—"

"Badger."

"Whatever." Imelda sighed. "I should've listened."

"And I shouldn't have ordered you about like that. I'm sorry."

Imelda regarded him silently with her golden eyes.

Finally, a small smile broke across her face.

"Don't feel too sorry. You made a pitiful badger."

Ambrose raised an eyebrow. "At least I didn't kiss one."

"That was an unpleasant shock."

"What? The kiss? Or the fact that the man in question turned out to be a badger?"

She looked at him strangely. "Does it matter?"

The question took Ambrose by surprise. Did it? If it was his own lips on hers, would she have shoved him away—or pulled him closer?

Yes, whispered a corner of his soul, at the same time that he replied gruffly:

"Not in the least."

Chapter 10

Imelda and Ambrose traveled the road until they found themselves at a lively inn that was not filled with cannibals but, rather, stuffed to the gills with happy, red-faced patrons who had traversed their own roads from far and wide to celebrate a wedding that they were not invited to but were hoping to sneak into nonetheless.

The day faded to evening, bringing us to the day of the wedding of the kingdom that so rudely refused to invite me.

Imelda and Ambrose have promised to retrieve my potion, but I can tell something is amiss. I can sniff their wants growing. Shifting, perhaps. But at the bottom of it is the lingering taste of Love's Keep fruit—freedom crisp as an apple, and just as sweet; belonging like a candy that never sours.

No sweet is truly sweet without the rich earth of bitterness.

And here is a bitterness they can't shake:

Lost, unremembered love.

It tastes like a wisp of smoke on the tongue.

Chapter 11

IMELDA

Imelda knew there was no freedom in love.

Every morning when she and her eleven sisters lined up in the hallway outside their bedroom, holding out their calloused and blistered feet for inspection, their ragged slippers dangling from their fingertips, their legs aching and their hair rumpled, their smiles vicious with their secret, her father would merely shake his head.

He was never mad that the slippers broke. He believed them when they said they had no idea how it happened. He was not, Imelda knew, a bad father.

He just worried.

"I had a sister who was lured into the woods, poisoned, and kept in a glass casket," he would tell them, as if somehow in the space of day and night, they had completely forgotten the story that had shaped their whole lives. "Do you know that I visited her grave for every birthday and left a slice of cake on the casket? She was so funny and lighthearted, and she was taken from me. My mother died of grief. My father went mad and married an ogress who tried to cook me! And my sister, when she finally woke, had changed. That casket had changed her, and she did not even stop by our home to collect her things or her favorite blanket before she married the king who had awoken her."

Her father would always sniff loudly, dabbing his eyes with the ends of his cloak.

"She never wrote, you know," he wept.

He would snap his fingers, and the court magicians would dutifully slip on the princesses' new slippers, each outfitted with a protective enchantment.

"I do this to keep you safe because I love you," her father would say mournfully.

The worst part was, Imelda believed him. She believed him when she ran too fast down the halls, only to be jerked back in mid-air because her father knew what she was doing and wished her to stop, for she might trip and fall and break something. She believed him when she paused too long in the mirror, pivoting on her heels to inspect her body as she grew older, only to be yanked forward because her father thought such displays unseemly for a lady. She believed him when she dragged her heels to every lesson, only to find herself suddenly speeding toward the classroom because her father insisted that a gently bred lady was never late.

The taste of Love's Keep fruit was a promise of freedom, which necessitated the absence of love. Up until now, that was all she'd wanted.

But the more time she spent around Ambrose, the more she had begun to realize that was not all she wanted.

She wanted his sometimes grim and brittle commentary. She wanted to laugh with him and make him laugh. She wanted him to steal glances at her the way she found herself doing with him.

And so, when she opened her door—they'd had separate rooms this time—and found Ambrose standing there, when she saw how his eyes widened at the sight of her, how his gaze fell to the floor and the faintest color touched his cheeks, when she discovered an answering shyness unfurling within her…she heard a warning:

This feeling will trap you. There is no freedom in this.

Imelda knew this… So then why was she so sad that their journey would soon end?

The inn where they had stayed lay at the end of a long, sloping meadow filled with nodding daisies beneath a late-afternoon spring sky. At the top of the meadow sat a golden door that had no hinges, next to a sign that read WEDDING ENTRANCE. The seemingly endless line of would-be guests had already disappeared through the door, whisked to the palace at the height of its wedding celebrations, and so she and Ambrose stood alone, staring at the doorknob.

We should go; otherwise, the stables will be full, and it would be in poor form to bring a horse inside a reception hall! tutted the cloak.

Ambrose and Imelda spoke at almost the same time.

"What's our plan?"

"I thought you had a plan!"

Ambrose pinched the bridge of his nose.

"We know that the queen—the *witch queen*—has a potion that turns people to statues," he began.

"Must endeavor not to break that," Imelda put in dryly.

"We know that the kingdom will let us in because we're—" Ambrose paused, gesturing between the two of them.

Stubborn? asked the cloak.

"No," Ambrose replied.

Foul-smelling?

"*NO.*"

Flesh-encased pillars of walking mortality?

"Do not make me turn you into glue because I—"

"Married," Imelda interrupted. "They'll let us in because they believe we're the married king and queen of Love's Keep."

Married! Congratulations!

Ambrose ignored it and continued, "After we're inside, we just have to get close enough to the witch queen. Then we'll grab the potion and make a run for it. Once we've found our way back and give it to the witch, we'll get what we want."

When Ambrose said that, his eyes lingered on her face. He was openly smiling. He had no plan. He didn't even have the right clothes for a wedding, though Imelda would never dream of saying that in front of the horse cloak. But it didn't matter. He didn't seem so much the stiff and stuffy man who had prowled the halls of Love's Keep. He seemed unburdened, adventurous even, and Imelda found herself smiling back.

Ambrose held out his arm. "Well? Shall we?"

Imelda took his arm gracefully. "With pleasure."

And she realized that she meant it.

⸺⸻

The moment they stepped through the door, they found themselves at the top of an opulent staircase, standing beneath the arching glass dome of a grand palace. A courtier dressed in golden livery waited to announce the line of guests. Five impressively dressed couples stood ahead of them. Rows of enchanted candles and pale white flowers netted over the thick crowd of merrymakers. Statues surrounded the circular room. Their hands were flung out, their eyes frozen wide with a wild panic now rendered in stone. Some of them huddled to the floor, arms clasped over their heads. Platters of iced cakes and cut fruit balanced on their still forms. Garlands of flowers draped their outstretched hands, and Imelda had the distinct impression that they had not started off as statues.

At the far end of the room sat the bride and groom. The bride was small and pale, her hands folded in her lap. Her groom was large and ruddy-faced with drink, one hand around his bride, the other gesturing for more wine.

Imelda scanned the crowd, a slow panic building inside her as she found the queen and king, located at the center of a throng of dancers. The witch queen had long, white hair that shimmered strangely. There was something familiar about it, though she knew she'd never seen this woman in her life. The witch queen wore a long, drab robe. She did not dance with her husband, who stood a short distance away from his wife. Imelda looked at the people who danced around her, circling her as if in a protective net. Imelda noticed the pinched look in their eyes and the strain in their mouths. As if they had no choice but to dance.

Something in her went cold at the sight.

How many times had she seen that expression on her sisters' faces as they ground their heels into the dirt, dragged their slippers over thorns, and hoped that they ripped in time for a touch of freedom? How many times had she seen that expression on her own face when she walked through the mirrored hallways of her father's palace, knowing that there was no place she could go that he wouldn't find her?

"I see her," Ambrose whispered.

"I do too."

I don't see anything, and also this is not a stable and I find it highly inappropriate that I am mixing with the guests.

The horse cloak whickered loudly, its hem ruffling up in irritation until Ambrose brushed it down.

When the witch queen raised her arm to cover her yawn, Imelda caught the twinkle of a vial kept near her wrist.

The stone potion.

By now, they were next in line for the courtier to announce their names. Imelda tapped the man's shoulder.

"Excuse me, but when will Her Royal Highness leave the dance floor for refreshment? My, uh, husband and I are far too exhausted to dance, but we still wish to pay our respects."

The courtier shook his head. "Awfully sorry, your highness, but the queen's life is far too precious for her to step out of the protective circle of her dancers. You may, of course, converse with her, and perhaps her response will be different once you speak."

Ambrose lightly touched Imelda's arm, and she drew back as the courtier announced them to the wedding party:

"King Ambrose and Queen Imelda of Love's Keep!"

The music abruptly stopped as the guests swiveled to face them. A familiar knot of cold rose up inside Imelda. She was used to this—the pitying stares, the troubadours who sang of them as the cursed king and queen, the halfhearted pats on her arm for her "tragic" life. Beside her, Ambrose fixed the crowd with a powerful stare, as if daring the guests to mock them.

Days ago, the whole world had known that their year and a day had come to an end, that they had failed to secure their place as monarchs of Love's Keep. The witch had promised to take care of that, and now Imelda wondered if she had failed at doing so. Honestly, she shouldn't have expected much out of someone who claimed to possess a "flamingo" purse. What *was* a flamingo? A rare and precious metal? The hide of some exotic dragon?

Imelda wanted to turn and run, but a second later, the ringing sound of applause filled her ears.

"Three cheers for the greatest love story of the ages!"

"To true love!"

"A most auspicious blessing indeed!"

Imelda and Ambrose exchanged a brief, bewildered gaze. Not knowing what else to do, Imelda curtsied, and Ambrose bowed, and together they descended the grand staircase toward the throng of dancers and the witch queen folded among them.

Imelda must have tightened her grip on Ambrose's arm because he turned to her, concern clear in his knitted brows.

"Are you all right?"

"Of course," Imelda responded, too quickly.

You do not seem all right.

Imelda ignored the horse cloak, as usual.

Ambrose lowered his voice. "It seems all we have to do is take up the next dance, and then we'll be close enough to—"

"Dance with someone else," she said hurriedly.

"What do you mean? I don't want to dance with anyone else."

Imelda looked at him sharply. Color touched Ambrose's cheeks.

"I mean, I shouldn't dance with anyone else. You're my—"

Lover! the cloak cut in happily.

"No."

Beloved across the spectrum of time!

"I—"

Mother of your unborn—

"QUEEN," Ambrose said loudly.

The cloak started to object, but Ambrose shooed it away.

"It's just...after that...that...rousing applause...it would look strange, don't you think? If we didn't dance together?"

Imelda stared at the crowd. "I suppose."

She did, on some level. But every other part of her screamed in protest. She did not dance unless she was totally alone. Around other people, dancing only reminded her that she was trapped, and she was free now, wasn't she?

Imelda lifted the hem of her gown an inch higher, sucking in her breath the moment she glimpsed her bare feet. No one to track her every move, to tell her where to go, to corner her in a hall and tell her to return to the stuffy rooms she hated, to remind her to do what she was told—

"Imelda?"

They were nearly at the bottom of the stairs. Imelda realized that she had gripped Ambrose's arm to the point where her knuckles had whitened.

"What's wrong?"

"I…I don't have good memories of dancing. I don't like it. Not anymore, at least."

Even the sensation of silk on her heels felt like chains.

"I don't have good memories of dances either," Ambrose said quietly.

"Always stepping on your partner's toes?" she asked.

"No."

Did your smell repel partners?

Ambrose ignored the horse cloak.

"The truth is that I'm quite good at dancing. I used to enjoy the music and the precision of every step. My brothers adored the dances for the charming women, and I have to admit, that certainly was one of the more enjoyable parts…but what I most loved was that every person had a place and a step and a position to fill. I loved how the music lulled you out of your own world, let you lose yourself to something greater. But things changed in my life…and the thought of losing myself to anything sounded terrifying." Ambrose faced her, holding out his hand, a look of determination flashing in his eyes. "But this time…this time I'm not scared."

Every place where Ambrose's gaze fell struck her like a fresh bruise, as if just by looking at her, he'd unearthed a tenderness she couldn't bear to touch. His words echoed in her mind: *"This time, I'm not scared."*

But Imelda was scared. She still felt that slow panic building inside her. But when her fingers met his, something eased away. A corner of her heart whispered soothingly: *He won't trap you; he won't keep you here.* Her pulse skittered, and her cheeks warmed when his hands slid around her waist, pulling her closer. This close, she could smell him. The *real* him, not the badger who wore his face and stole a kiss. He smelled like the meadow they had crossed to get here, like the vast pines that bowed overhead when they walked through the woods. Like something that could not be trapped in a fist. His chest was solid with muscle, and he fit her to him as if it were the most natural thing in the world. She closed her eyes as the music swept over her.

Ambrose hadn't lied.

He *was* a good dancer.

Light on his feet, as if tempting the music to chase him. Her bones seemed to expand in her chest. Every new breath she sucked in chafed a bit, like she had never breathed properly until now. And Imelda realized with growing wonder and alarm that it was here—clasped tightly in the arms of someone she had grown to trust, someone who made her laugh and who had fought his own imprisonments—that she finally felt free.

Chapter 12

AMBROSE

Ambrose knew there was no trust in love.

Love made no promise to stay, to put down roots. It could always be taken from you. It was one of the few things in life he believed with certainty. Even love you didn't remember possessing could be taken from you, and so the best thing one could cultivate when faced with such an emotion was distance.

Ambrose had learned this lesson young. He was the middle child, sandwiched between cold and determined Ulrich and handsome and grinning Octavius. Their mother, who was fair and lovely and young, had never had the chance to be anything but.

When she died, the brothers mourned, and not knowing where to turn, they turned to each other. Ambrose remembered a time when they pushed their beds together so they could sleep side by side, when one of them refused to start eating if their trio was incomplete. If their father grew angry with one, the other two would leap up to take the blame. With his brothers beside him, Ambrose felt quite invincible.

Until it ended.

They were eighteen, seventeen, and sixteen. By then, adulthood had descended upon them like night. The world grew darker, shapes once familiar blurred into unknown entities, and all of it had happened so slowly that Ambrose hadn't even realized his eyes had adjusted to the dark.

Until eighteen, the three brothers had assumed that Ulrich, the eldest, would take the throne. But then their father announced that the throne would in fact go to the brother he deemed the most deserving. It was a strange shift, one that Ambrose didn't know what to do with. Was he supposed to want the throne? What if he didn't?

The evening of the announcement, he found his younger brother waiting for him in the library, two amber-colored drinks gleaming before him. Ambrose would never forget how his youngest brother turned to him, the smile he'd fixed on his face that looked no different from any of his smiles in the past. He would not forget how tightly Octavius hugged him, and how relieved Ambrose had felt that nothing would change.

Octavius had held out his glass. "To new changes, brother."

Ambrose clinked his glass to his, then knocked it back. The world blurred, and he fell to the ground. When he came to, it had turned to night outside, and he was lying in the healer's chamber. He later found out he would have died if he had taken just a sip more of poison.

The next day, he had moved to a new bedchamber. He feigned ignorance when Octavius approached him with something like shame in his eyes. Ambrose took his love, and he put distance between himself and it, and in this way, he survived.

Distance, he thought, was crucial.

He knew this, which was why he felt lightheaded when he danced with Imelda. It was dangerous to hold her this close, and he'd known it for some time. He'd never admitted this to Imelda, but once he'd seen her dancing in Love's Keep. She thought she was alone, for she moved so freely. So happily. He'd watched her a moment too long, all too aware of the length of her limbs and the fierce joy in her eyes. And he knew, right there and then, that she could hurt him.

So what was he doing?

He spun Imelda in a circle, pulling her closer, inhaling the strange, smoky scent of her. Every part of Imelda burned with life— from the feral curls of hair to the flash of amber fire in her eyes, the startling heat of her skin, and the frantic thrum of her heart, like a bird beating its wings against a cage, desperate for flight.

Soon, this would end.

He might be dancing with Imelda, but he hadn't forgotten why.

The witch queen, and her potions, drew closer to them with every expert twist and twirl, sidestep, and spin. Soon, Imelda would release him, and that distance would rush back in like a wave. But for these next few heartbeats, he didn't have to let go. He brought her even closer, lowering his head to her now-upturned face. Imelda inhaled sharply, sucking on her lower lip. Lightning flashed through his body. The moment he looked at her, Imelda's eyes fluttered shut.

Look at me, he willed.

Ambrose hadn't realized that over the years, he'd made himself a ghost. All this time, the fear of losing anything had left him with nothing, and the world had never felt so real until Imelda marched into it, refusing to stay out of the way. Now, when she closed her eyes, he might as well have been snipped out of existence.

Look at me, he willed once more. *Don't make me invisible.*

As if she'd heard him, Imelda's eyes flew open.

They beheld each other.

For one moment, the candlelight conspired to render them unfamiliar to the other. For one moment, they were no longer the tragic king and queen of Love's Keep, but just Imelda and Ambrose, two strangers whose lives had knitted together for the length of a song. Two people so used to walking that sly line between defeat and expectation that to stumble across one another felt like they had blindfolded Fate and turned her about the room, setting her loose upon some other unfortunate soul while they drank the other in and knew, without a shadow of a doubt, that this was exactly where they wished to stand.

"I *know* you!" an unfamiliar voice proclaimed.

The moment broke.

Ambrose felt Fate reasserting itself. His hands jerked back from Imelda's body as if pulled on by invisible strings. When the witch queen stepped into their midst, Ambrose felt all of Imelda's borrowed vibrancy falling away from him. He was half a ghost once more.

Imelda swiveled toward the witch queen, her eyes widening.

The revelers paused, and the music stopped once more. The circle of dancers around the witch queen jerked back like puppets. The king, who Ambrose had realized was little more than a prop wielded by his wife, eyed Imelda warily. The witch queen stepped forward, and Ambrose could see her clearly now.

She was tall and pale, with a thin nose and a shrewd mouth and—he realized with a lurch—*Imelda's* eyes. That exact shade of honey, and tilted like a fey's. It was saying something that he'd noticed her eyes before her strange, uncanny hair, which caught the light of the candles and refracted it into rainbows.

The witch queen's hair was made of individual strands of glass.

"You are my brother's daughter, aren't you, child? One of my twelve dancing nieces, I presume?"

Imelda stared at her, quickly recovering. "You're…you're the sister who got lured away… Father said you slept in that glass casket for ages…"

The witch queen smiled, tossing her hair back over her shoulder. It clinked like wind chimes.

"My brother always was too cautious for his own good. I *chose* that casket. It was a trade: Sleep…for *magic*."

With that, she lifted her sleeve, showing off the potions stitched to the cuff of her gown. When she raised her arm, a shudder ran through the guests. The king paled, and someone whimpered.

Ambrose wished he could just take his dagger, slash off a potion, and run, but Imelda's eyes went wide. She was practically quivering with questions. He could see them burning inside her.

If he caused a commotion and forced them to flee, she'd never forgive him.

And judging by the witch queen's power, he couldn't even be sure they'd get too far.

"Let us talk, shall we, niece? We are long overdue for a family reunion…"

Imelda looked over her shoulder, turning to Ambrose.

The queen regarded him, her smile a bloodless slash on her face.

"Your beloved may join, of course. Come, nephew. Follow me."

The queen snapped her fingers, and the wedding party continued. The candles flickered overhead as he followed the queen and Imelda into the shadowed halls of the castle.

The horse cloak snorted and neighed.

Extract thy sword, and we shall charge upon the crowd and trample the queen!

"No."

Very well… Let me charge upon the crowd and trample the queen!

"No!"

But Imelda—

"Knows what she's doing," Ambrose said quickly.

He took off the cloak.

How rude—

Ambrose switched the cloak inside out and clasped it back around his neck, muffling the horse cloak's newest rant.

He hoped he hadn't made a liar of himself. The way Imelda was looking at the witch queen, with something like wonder in her eyes, made him uneasy. The witch queen led them away from the reception hall, down a corridor lined by torches. The moment they passed a torch, the light guttered out behind them. All the while, the potions clinked together around the cuff of her sleeve.

Ambrose had grown used to Imelda's constant chatter, and her abrupt silence worried him. He wanted to look into her face, but the passage was too narrow for them to walk side by side, concealing her expression entirely.

"My father—" Imelda started hesitantly.

"Was a sweet little fool, if I recall correctly." The witch queen laughed dismissively. "I did like him, though. He always did my bidding, rather like a puppy."

"He used to watch over me and my sisters fiercely," Imelda said defensively. "Because he loved us…and because he loved *you*. He thought you were stolen away from them, forced to sleep in that casket until a king kissed you—"

"Posh and nonsense." The witch queen laughed again. "But I had to feed that lie to my family, or else they never would have understood why I sought something more than what my little kingdom had to offer. I wanted the husband, the throne, the adoring subjects, I suppose...but I also wanted power. And I knew how to get it. Power likes a sacrifice. My sleep, my youth, my childhood... for knowledge."

"But you're the reason why—"

The witch queen whirled around. "*I* am the reason why *I* am free. Can you say the same for yourself, child?"

Imelda said nothing.

By then, the hallway had come to an end in a rotunda lined with seven statues. Behind four of the statues gleamed bright gold doors. Behind the other three statues lay shadow-darkened passages. The sound of rushing water reached Ambrose's ears, along with the scent of stale air.

The witch queen gestured to one of the statues.

"Luckily for you, *that* will never be your fate. It doesn't work on our bloodline—at least not for more than an hour or so. And I never harm one of my own."

Ambrose suppressed a shudder. "How lucky, indeed."

The witch queen startled, turning to him as if she'd forgotten he was there.

"You would not be so lucky."

"I...I'd like to talk to you about how to..." Imelda began.

"How to be like me?"

"Yes."

Ambrose felt his heart sinking into his stomach. The witch queen's smile never changed its shape as she held out her hand to Imelda. Ambrose watched, waiting for some telltale flicker or hesitation in Imelda's body, but she didn't waver as she took her aunt's hand, and she didn't turn to face him either.

"Why don't you have a look around?" Imelda said. "I might be a while."

The two of them disappeared down a hallway to the right. Ambrose stared into the hallway long after it was clear that Imelda wasn't coming back. *And why should she?* he thought. Her dream was freedom, not...he refused to finish his thought. When they had danced, he had only thought of putting distance between them, but it seemed Imelda had beaten him to it.

He should have been relieved, but all he felt was loss.

Alone and feeling increasingly foolish, Ambrose shook loose his cloak. It spluttered at him.

Undignified for a steed such as myself! You should be very glad that the witch queen was blind to my magnificent form and deaf to my loud hooves.

"My apologies."

Now do we trample the queen—?

"Now we figure out a way to get one of those potions on our own and then escape. Every second we spend here is a second we could turn into statues."

I have always dreamed of my likeness being rendered in stone. I cannot wait to admire it!

Ambrose did not bother to correct the cloak. If he was right about the sound of rushing water, then one of the two hallways would be an exit. Ambrose walked down the first and found himself in an empty dining room, lit with torches held aloft in the hands of wide-eyed statues.

It seems as though we are escaping, but what about Imelda?

"She is staying here."

No, she isn't.

"Yes, she is."

But she told us to have a look around—

"She doesn't want anything to do with us anymore, trust me."

Down the second hallway, the sound of rushing water grew louder and louder, the passage opening up into a small, covered dock. Huge crates stuffed with straw and hay lay stacked by the water's shore, forming tall rows that stretched to the very edge of the dock. Ambrose tried to peer into one of the crates, but it was pitch black and sealed with wax. From the mouth of the hall, Ambrose spotted narrow barges bobbing in the water. He took a couple of steps forward, peering out from behind one of the rows of crates. The channel flowed out to join a river. As it wasn't quite nightfall yet, Ambrose could see the distant shapes of hills and forests.

Out of the corner of his eye, Ambrose caught the splayed shadow of an approaching figure. He drew farther back into the hall, but not so far that he couldn't catch the man's loud and persistent grumbling.

"…Who bothers with shipments on a wedding day? Honestly! I'm sure all the other cursed kingdoms could wait before they received their little…"

The man's words trailed into silence as he moved farther away once more. Ambrose edged along the walls, scooting back toward the rotunda. The horse cloak coughed slightly.

So our plan is that we shall trample this man and then…

"Escape," Ambrose whispered.

At least now he knew how to leave and where to go, but it was pointless without the witch queen's potion. There were still the bedrooms to check. And the dining room hadn't been properly explored. Maybe if he…

The sound of distant footsteps made him straighten. It wasn't coming from the dock, but somewhere in the darkened rotunda.

Now we trample?

A figure sped toward him, and Ambrose reached for his sword—

"Got it!" Imelda yelled.

"What?"

The sight of Imelda stunned him. She was practically flying down the hall toward him, two vials of potion clutched to her chest, her bare feet kicking up the ends of her full skirt. That wild expression he'd come to associate with her spread across her face— lioness eyes wide with the thrill of skirting danger, cheeks flushed with breathlessness, curls tumbling around her.

Distance, he reminded himself.

But he could not make himself step back as she closed the space between them, finally coming to a stop before him.

"You came back," he said.

Imelda stared at him, then frowned and waved the potions wildly in his face.

"Did you hit your head? Let's go! I got the potion. Managed to use one on her, but who knows how long it will hold. This place is worse than the inn with the cannibals. Please tell me you did what I asked and found a way out?"

Dimly, Ambrose remembered Imelda's offhand comment: *"Why don't you have a look around."* He was a fool. But he was a happy fool because he'd been wrong the whole time, and a painful joy needled up behind his ribs.

"I—"

More footsteps. Louder, this time. Angry shouts reached them at the end of the hall.

Trample now?

Imelda grabbed Ambrose's hand, and they sprinted toward the dock, jumping onto the closest barge they could find. The boat rocked beneath them, pitching him forward. Ambrose clung to the boat's edge and stared into the dark water.

Just below the reach of the oars stood an underwater grove full of statues with outstretched hands. Weeds wrapped around their throats and fingers; pale crabs scuttled through their flung-open mouths and made homes in the ruins of their teeth.

"We have to go! *Now!*" shouted Imelda.

The barge was tied to the one before it, and Ambrose lunged forward with his short dagger, making quick work of the knots tethering them in place. The dockworker Ambrose had seen was starting to shuffle toward them. Ambrose and Imelda hunkered down into the bottom of the barge. Any moment now, the guards would burst through and find them, and most likely, Ambrose would end up frozen just like the others.

"Maybe we should swim out or—"

There was a popping sound.

Ambrose stiffened as he swiveled his head. Imelda had unstoppered one of the potions.

"What the hell are you doing?"

"Getting us out of here. My aunt said that she ships out the statues. Just pretend it was an urgent order."

"You can't be serious!"

"It doesn't work on her own blood. I'm her own blood—ergo, it won't work on me. At least, not forever. It's our only chance to get out of here."

"Don't!"

"Don't tell me what to do!"

The horse cloak sighed. *So we are not trampling.*

"But what if you stay that way? What if you don't come back?"

Imelda paused. Was that a slight flush coloring her cheeks?

"I can't imagine why I'd stay away," she said softly.

There was something in how she said it, a softness to her voice he'd never heard before. Before he could ask another question, she knocked back the whole potion, shuddering a bit. "Ugh. Tastes like rocks."

A tinge of gray worked its way up from her feet, netting across her dress.

A door slammed in the distance. Then another. Cold rushed through Ambrose's heart. The guards must have cleared the dining room and were now checking the bedrooms, looking for them.

"Oy!" Ambrose yelled. "Queen sent me on an urgent journey to deliver one of these."

He looked over his shoulder, something catching in his throat as he realized that Imelda had fully turned to stone. Her smile, coy and slightly pouting, looked lifeless and each of her wayward curls eerily chiseled.

"But the crate!" the dockworker protested.

"It's a special mission," Ambrose said hurriedly.

He pushed the oar into the water. The soldiers had slammed the last door and were hurrying down the steps of the hall. He grimaced as the bottom of his oar struck the side of a statue.

The barge sailed silently forward.

Ambrose heard a soldier yell, "Stop!" and pushed faster.

The opening of the river channel brightened before him. One more push and they were free, caught by the river's current and borne far away from this bizarre kingdom. His pulse pounded through him, but not because they'd escaped…

But because he couldn't stop thinking of Imelda's face and the last words she'd uttered to him: *"I can't imagine why I'd stay away."*

They were nothing but a handful of words, but to Ambrose, they'd roped him in, closing up the last of the distance he'd tried to put between them.

Chapter 13

AMBROSE

Ambrose watched the castle pull away from them with every stroke of the oar. Hours passed as the current swirled beneath the boat, the water ahead now draped in heavy mists. The smell of village woodsmoke reached him, and hunger scratched at his stomach.

Ambrose risked a glance over his shoulder. It was far too strange to see Imelda stretched out like that, hair fanned about her, lips frozen in that coy smile, her hands strategically folded around the remaining stone potion so that it could not be taken from her. He found himself unaccountably furious with her. What she'd done was brave and reckless, but that wasn't what made him angry. It was her stillness when he burned to ask her questions.

What did she mean, *"I can't imagine why I'd stay away"*?

Did that mean what he thought it meant?

Ambrose shook his head, trying to clear out the multitude of foolish questions boiling inside him.

The cloak sighed and asked in a small voice, *Did I perform poorly? Is that why Imelda is a statue and not talking to us?*

Perhaps a few days ago, Ambrose would've informed the cloak that it was not, in fact, a horse. But it was as if Imelda's glare worked through stone, and he found himself saying:

"You performed quite admirably. Best, er, horse I've ever encountered."

Really?

"Truly."

Well. I knew that, of course, but noble steeds must be modest.

Ambrose smiled to himself, and then he sat back, letting the river pull them onward.

⁓

Some time later, they came upon a small millhouse seated beside a squat little pub, with a tiny dock jutting out from the grassy yard. Ambrose tied the boat to one of the stands, then carefully hauled Imelda onto the wooden platform.

Ambrose threw the cloak around Imelda's shoulders, feeling his face slightly warm when he tied it about her throat.

"In case you get cold or something," he muttered.

Oh, look at him. Talking to a statue and a cloak? Ambrose pinched the bridge of his nose before taking stock of where they'd ended up. A quaint village sprawled out ahead of them, lantern lights and small fires casting golden warmth against the windows. It was full night—cold stars knitted above them, and a silver moon cast pale threads across the water.

Imelda would have found it beautiful, but she couldn't see it.

"Wake up."

Ambrose reached out almost shyly, tracing the stone embroidery across her shoulder.

"Please?"

Nothing.

Imelda had been like this the whole time, and it was starting to make him nervous. She had been so sure that the potion wouldn't keep because of her bloodline. It was supposed to wear off in an hour, but more time had passed, and what if she was wrong?

He leaned forward, inspecting her a little closer. In the moonlight, her stone eyelashes cast spiked shadows onto her cheeks. She looked mysterious and terribly beautiful, like a precious treasure scurried out from a temple, the hum of ancient stories knocking against her teeth and ready to be unlocked by a single—

Are you going to kiss her?

Ambrose startled backward. "Of course not."

She would hit you.

Very true.

"I was just trying to see if there were any signs of life, that's all," Ambrose told the cloak.

The cloak tightened around Imelda's shoulders protectively, then batted at Ambrose's hand.

"Ow!"

She would want me to do that.

The cloak snuggled around Imelda more tightly.

"Let's just get somewhere safe for the night and deal with this in the morning."

Ambrose hauled Imelda and the horse cloak through the back end of the pub's alley. Discarded shellfish and peeled, rotting fruits littered both sides. At the far end lay a narrow, trampled grass pathway that curved up the side of a hill and came to rest beneath a copse of moonlit trees where they could easily make camp until the morning.

Imelda, it turned out, was extraordinarily heavy.

Just then, the door to the pub swung open and a kitchen boy called out: *"William! You're needed in the bar!"*

Unfortunately, Ambrose was right in the middle of dragging a very rough and heavy Imelda past the door, and growling, "Gods, you're hard."

"Um, never mind, then—"

"Wait, it's not what you think!"

"Just come in when you're finished!"

"I'm with a statue!"

There was a heavy pause behind the door, and then it slammed decisively shut.

"Not...like that..." Ambrose protested weakly.

Soon, Ambrose had dragged Imelda up the hill, positioning her under a tree. The horse cloak immediately began to snore, leaving Ambrose alone with his thoughts. He stared up at Imelda, and his heart sank.

The witch queen had been so sure that the potion wouldn't work on her bloodline, but clearly, she was wrong.

Which meant Imelda was...*gone*.

Silver light limned her face and hair, and Ambrose felt a chasm of panic opening up inside him.

For a year and a day, he'd squandered the chance to know her, and now their days together had drawn to a close without him knowing. Only now, when it was too late, did he realize how much he wanted to know her, *truly* know her. He wanted to deserve a secret smile from her, to watch as she kicked off every pair of shoes, to hear her sigh whenever the sky looked fire-dipped and stole her breath, to bury his face in her neck and drink in that smoky scent of her and know she wouldn't singe him.

He stared at the ground. All the things he hadn't said—and now, never could—bubbled up in his chest.

"I have something to confess..." Ambrose said aloud. "A part of me never believed that the witch could steal what I felt forever.

I knew it the moment I stumbled in on you dancing alone, three months into our reign—if you could call it that—at Love's Keep. All that time, I'd avoided looking too closely at you, and then all of a sudden…I couldn't stop." He took a deep breath. "I'd never seen eyes like yours, or wild joy like yours. And I wanted so badly to be part of your life…and that terrified me. *You* terrified me, Imelda. I knew, in some hidden corner of myself, that I could fall in love with you again. I had survived the loss of love once, but what if I couldn't do it again?"

Ambrose gulped down the night air, hoping the starlight would fortify his words.

"I used to refuse holding on to anything because I knew I could lose it. But if I could relive this past year and a day, I would take that chance… You once said you hated being tied to the ground and that if you ever wore a pair of shoes, you'd only consent to a pair that let you fly instead of holding you down. I never want to hold you down, Imelda. All I want is for you to want to come back to me. Whether you run or fly. It doesn't matter."

Ambrose looked up at the Imelda statue, half hoping and half dreading that his foolish speech would resurrect her.

But she was as implacable as stone.

And eventually, he fell asleep.

———

The next morning, he woke up to the sunlight streaming on his face and something rough tickling the edge of his nose. The horse cloak.

I just realized I never get hungry. Do you think that's normal for horses?

Ambrose jolted upright, and the horse cloak, which had been

thrown over him like a blanket, tumbled in a huff of irritation to the ground.

Brightness slanted into his eyes. Imelda stood still as a statue, but...she wasn't a statue anymore. She pushed her hair back, sunlight pouring out of her hands as she used the last of the enchanted road that was to lead them to the final place where the witch would meet them once more. Ambrose couldn't stop staring at her. She was back. She was *back*.

She startled when she noticed he'd woken up. Something like panic flickered behind her eyes.

"Hello," she breathed.

Her smile was soft and uncertain. She was looking at him funny, and Ambrose scrubbed at his face self-consciously.

"You're not a statue anymore."

"Surprise."

In a rush, Ambrose remembered all the things he'd said...the way he'd looked at her when he thought he'd never see her again.

"Uh, and how was that experience?"

"Are you asking me if I enjoyed being a statue?"

"...Yes."

"Did you enjoy being a beaver?"

"Badger."

"Whatever."

"I remember some advantages..." He paused. "What do you remember?"

"Nothing." She paused. "Is there something I should remember?"

"Not at all."

They looked at each other.

The last of the road had spun out through the woods, and

Ambrose felt an unfamiliar ache settling behind his ribs. This might be their last day and night. Before them, the road stretched out like a shining thread of hope.

Imelda gestured ahead. "Shall we? The rest of our lives awaits us."

The rest of their lives. *Strange*, he thought as he gathered his things and fell into step beside Imelda.

When they'd started this journey, all he'd wanted was what he'd seen in that bite of fruit from the long-dead tree of Love's Keep.

Place, power, certainty.

But then Imelda stole a glance at him beneath her lashes, and Ambrose felt that terrible gnaw starting at the base of his heart.

That wasn't all he wanted anymore.

Chapter 14

IMELDA

Imelda had lied.

Not a huge lie...but not a little one either.

For the most part, when she'd been turned to stone, she could *sense* life around her, but she herself felt pleasantly weighed down, her soul tucked into the rock like a sleeping jewel. But as the magic had worn away, her senses had stumbled back to her little by little.

She sensed Ambrose first.

Her eyes were seamed shut, but she *felt* him. The warmth of him, the distant pressure of his palms propping her up. She heard him speaking, but the words dragged in and out until one phrase gleamed bright as an anchor and she held it tight:

"I could fall in love with you again."

When she shook off the dregs of the magic, Ambrose was fast asleep and scowling, and whatever else he might have said had long since dissolved into the night air.

"I could fall in love with you again."

Those words terrified and thrilled her in equal measure.

Imelda was not as young as she used to be, and she no longer lied to herself. Something had changed over the past week. She knew she was not in love. But she also knew she was standing at the threshold of something she hadn't felt before. Her heart peered over a chasm, not knowing whether there was light or darkness at the end of it all.

She thought this kind of feeling would be like shackles weighing her down with every step. But Ambrose made her feel weightless. He could be thoughtful and quiet, funny and sly. He listened to her in a way no one else ever had. And when he held her—whether it was jumping from a window or spinning into a dance—Imelda didn't just feel free in his arms. She felt *safe*.

Several times she'd caught herself turning to him as they walked in awkward silence down the enchanted road. Each time, she stopped herself from speaking. What would she say anyway? *I heard you might want to love me again, and that seems like not so terrible a thing?* Several times she'd worked up the courage to say just that, but a cold voice held her back.

And it was not her own.

Right before she'd stolen the witch queen's stone potion, her aunt had looked her in the eye and flashed her thin and terrible smile.

"Trust me, child, he will try to control you, in the end. I know what you want, and the only way to get it is through power. Soon enough, you'll see. He'll just try to keep you down, and then what will you do? Better to look out for yourself, to love only *yourself."*

"Are you all right?"

Imelda glowered. She felt unaccountably angry at him. Angry that he'd made her feel this. Angry, still, that she didn't know what to do next.

"Ah, then I suppose you really did like being a statue."

"What?" Imelda snapped.

"I've never seen you so silent. We're practically there."

Ahead, the enchanted road sloped into a valley surrounded by golden hills. The town was less than an hour's walk away and looked *almost* ordinary. There was a tiny castle, ribbons of houses, and a river flowing through the middle. But the whole thing was completely enclosed by a glass sphere. Flurries of snow drifted past the crystal globe, and frost webbed its way across the surface, like a bowl of winter had toppled over and trapped the town beneath it. Meanwhile, autumn painted the earth outside in streaks of gold.

"How strange," Imelda said, awestruck.

"That women would rather be statues than suffer my company? Because I was thinking that was more harsh than strange."

"Oh, stop rooting around for a compliment."

"Toss me one and I'll stop searching."

Imelda looked at him. Autumn light had picked out the bronze undertones of his skin, turned his dark hair lustrous, and softened the hard set of his mouth. Or maybe that was just his smile, which he'd brought out more and more lately. Her pulse quickened.

"For example," he said magnanimously, "'Ambrose, you are as fair as the day is long.'"

The day is almost over, the horse cloak contributed.

Ambrose swatted at the hem, and a laugh snuck out of her throat.

"Or 'Ambrose, you make an exceptional beaver.'"

"Badger."

"Perhaps 'Ambrose, thank you for hauling me through God knows where while I was a piece of rock.'"

"Fine," Imelda groaned. "Thank you."

Ambrose grinned, and they passed the rest of the hour in a silence that wasn't stiff or awkward but heavy and, honestly, sad. With each minute, Imelda realized, they were getting closer to the last. The witch would meet them soon, they would hand her the potion, and she, in turn, would give them that which they most desired. The flavor of the fruit of Love's Keep ghosted across her tongue, promising her freedom and a life spent chasing all her wants. It's just that, somehow, her wants had also taken the shape of someone she hadn't expected.

"Today is our last day," said Imelda.

"Is that what has you so grumpy?"

"I'm just tired, is all."

A look of pain crossed Ambrose's face, but he smiled.

"Either way, I promise not to waste it."

The moment Imelda and Ambrose crossed the bridge leading to the snowy town, wintry magic wrapped around them. On the other side of the bridge stood a huge, ice-rimmed castle. Villagers crowded its sprawling lawn. Every few feet, there appeared a magical wonder. Imelda spied an entrance to a garden made entirely of glass. A towering, eight-foot-high merchant wearing a trailing, iridescent coat full of pockets shouted out his wares for sale:

"Angel lilies! Seedlings for unicorns! Truth mirrors and more are here to find! Just let me take a peek inside your mind!"

Strings of frosty lights crisscrossed above them. A carousel of ice and glass floated over the ground, its carved crystalline horses and gryphons leaping off their posts and gallivanting around the palace before settling once more onto their podium when a likely customer ventured past.

Fake! the horse cloak cried when it saw them.

A porter cheerfully handed them a map.

"Welcome to our cursed little town! Behind me, you'll find

the famous palace with our sleeping princess guarded by a dragon! Beware, if you cross the tenth step, you will likely die! Just on the other side of the castle lies our cozy inn featuring home-cooked meals and feather-down beds. And *here*, you'll find our family-friendly tourist attractions!"

"Your town is…cursed?" Ambrose said.

"Oh yes. None of us can leave this eternal winter until the princess wakes up. Minus the tourists, of course. But that's all right. So far, it's been a boon to our local economy. Enjoy!"

Imelda watched as the porter gently shooed them toward the lawn so that he could greet the next people in line. Imelda shivered, warming her arms, and then frowned. Ambrose had taken off down the row of tents, his cloak billowing behind him and his hands in his pockets.

"What are you doing!" she called.

Ambrose glanced over his shoulder. His gray eyes looked bright even as his mouth twisted in sorrow.

"Doing as the gentleman bade us to do and *enjoying*. You're welcome to continue your best impersonation of a statue—"

Imelda scowled.

"Or you could join me and have some fun."

"As if you know how to have any kind of fun."

"I have quite the imagination."

Imelda didn't miss the way his voice went a little rough when he said that. She also didn't miss the sudden rabbit-quick pulse of her heart.

"As if you're not curious enough to find out whether that's true." Ambrose raised an eyebrow. "For an adventurous princess, you're turning out to be exceptionally boring—"

"I am no such thing!"

He smirked. "Prove it."

Imelda watched for an excruciatingly long second as he walked off into the crowds. And then she took after him, determined to prove him wrong.

———∽

Let me show you what *I* see. Sometimes magic is too vast to comprehend up close and demands that you step back and *back*, until you believe that the sky is a length of blue silk you might wrap around your wrist and then forget all about. That is the perspective needed to witness an intrusion of love, for it is no different than magic.

See how he watches the frost spangle in her hair like diamonds; hear how she laughs until she's out of breath. Watch the impossible chasm of an inch between their fingers as their skin flirts with the idea of touch and their minds pretend to be full of snow. You can trace the edge of nighttime, the heavy curtain of dusk, the way it weighs their every step.

One night.

Last night.

One night after a year and a day of wasted nights, and she smells of smoke, and his eyes look like poured silver, and her laugh is costlier than coffers of gold, and if he spends it all in one night...ah, at least he possessed it for an evening. As for her, her skin feels too tight. She wants freedom, yes, and abandonment, and in the snow slanting across his smile, she finds one, and in the breadth of his shoulders and too-dark eyes, she sees the promise of the latter. You think it's lust, but it's not. It's bravery. To close distances. To take the raw, beating part of you and hold it up to the light. And the purpose of quests is, naturally, to do brave things.

And now...

Now...

Now, they stand at their respective doors. Now, the hall is dark, and the night fully ripe. Now, we really have no business watching, but we all crave magic, so...

Chapter 15

IMELDA

Imelda leaned against the door of her bedroom, which shared a door with Ambrose's room. They had eaten, washed, and tucked the horse cloak onto a round peg and now stood around, on the verge of saying goodnight and shutting their doors.

The wind blew sugary puffs of snow against the night-dark windowpanes. The noise in the halls had stuttered off into silence, and tomorrow seemed as far away as a new century. And yet she knew that wasn't true. Tomorrow, the witch would come and hand them the very thing they wished for, and all of this would soon become a distant dream.

Ambrose looked at her, the full force of those gray eyes practically pinning her into place. His hair was still damp and slightly curled about his ears. The undershirt he'd worn had been reduced to tatters, so he'd purchased a new one that made no effort to conceal the broadness of his shoulders or the lean muscles roping his arms.

"What are you thinking about?"

Ambrose did not hesitate. "You."

He stood a good five feet away from her. But the moment he said that, she imagined she could hear that word pressed to her mouth. Her neck. Everywhere.

"What about me?"

"The things I've learned about you," he said quietly.

"Such as?"

"For one, you make a terrible statue—"

"I shall mourn that till the end of my days."

"You detest shoes because they anchor you to one place. I've never seen you wield a hairbrush, but I imagine that would be a fearsome sight to behold. You could find a reason to laugh at practically anything in the world. And you're brave to the point where I worry about your sense of self-preservation."

It wasn't enough for her to smile at that. Her whole body seemed to join in the effort, a warm glow spreading up from her toes. With every unfurling of warmth, Imelda felt an answer loosening. Since her encounter with the witch queen, she hadn't been able to shake off her aunt's warning: *"Trust me, child, he will try to control you, in the end."*

She couldn't tell what was the brave thing to do with that warning. Her aunt said that power came only from control. But Imelda didn't want her aunt's bloodless, glassy power. She wanted the power that came from *living*, breathing things, not a life lived as a cold, unyielding statue. She might get hurt. She might get rejected outright. But at least she tried…and wasn't that the truest sense of bravery? To open one's eyes in the dark and step forward anyway?

Imelda found her voice. "Is that all?"

Perhaps there was something in the way she said it because Ambrose's head jerked up sharply. He gave her an assessing look, his dark brows knitted close, cruel mouth shaped in an uncertain smile.

"And you hate being commanded."

Imelda's smile turned coy.

"True. I always find myself compelled to do the exact opposite of a thing."

Ambrose looked down at the ground, holding himself stiffly. The room shifted around them. If it was possible, the night seemed to have gotten darker and more distant, the hall more silent, the space between them burning with invisible flames. Imelda held her breath until Ambrose looked up and finally said:

"Then don't come near me."

She took a step. Then two. Hardly believing herself. They were a handspan distance from each other.

"Don't…" His eyes found hers. "Don't touch me."

Imelda laid her palms to his chest, feeling the wild beating of his heart. She closed her eyes for a moment, imagining that this wasn't their last day but their first, and how different things might have been. She slid her palms up, lacing them around his neck, savoring the sharp intake of his breath. His hands went around her waist, firm and hot against her skin. He lowered his head, his lips grazing the slope of her neck.

"Imelda, I beg you…don't kiss me."

Imelda turned her face toward his and did the exact opposite of what he'd commanded. She kissed him deeply, heat searing through her body at the low growl in his chest when her mouth moved from his lips to the base of his throat. His hands skimmed up her body, trailing heat in their wake until his fingers paused at the stays of her bodice. Imelda undid them slowly, watching as his eyes darkened and his breaths turned shallow. The dress slid from her shoulders, pooling around her ankles. The moment she reached for Ambrose, he grabbed her to him, and they fell onto the bed.

Well, what do *you* think happened?
Don't look!
Bah!
So rude.

Chapter 16

AMBROSE

Ambrose couldn't stop grinning as he walked back from the magical, snow-filled markets. It had taken him a good two hours to find the right gift, but he held it in his hands, and he knew it was perfect.

As he walked back to the inn, he replayed every moment with Imelda. He could hardly sleep for the sensation of lying beside her. Her wild hair got everywhere, tickling his skin. In sleep, she kicked a bit. Sometimes she'd nuzzle against him, other times roll into a tight, furious ball. She stole the covers. She drooled a bit. And Ambrose felt an ache rising up in his heart because he couldn't wait for every night to follow. He couldn't wait to *know* her. To know how she took her tea. What flowers made her sneeze. Whether she would always laugh a little after lovemaking, as if she were amused by her own happiness.

And it was that thought that had sent him out into the market without a cloak, his whole body flaming at the promise of today and the next day, and the day after that. He tried practicing what he would say.

"Imelda, will you be my wife…still? No, that's awful. Imelda, could we have another go at this? Far too casual. Imelda, would you—"

"Excuse me, sir?"

Ambrose turned around to see the porter at his elbow. "There's a raven message for you, sir."

Ambrose frowned, looking down at the parcel in his hand. He wanted to rush upstairs, wake Imelda, tell her everything that weighed on his heart, and then spend the rest of the morning and afternoon in that bed with her while they waited on the witch.

But that wouldn't do.

"I'll…I'll be right there. Just let me, ah, put this away."

Ambrose headed up the stairs, his heart still light. He could picture it perfectly: their place of power restored at Love's Keep, the white tree in bloom, the shocked look on his brothers' faces. Imelda smiling freely. The life they should have had from the start finally resuming course.

Ambrose pushed open the door to his room. Imelda was still fast asleep. In the armoire, the horse cloak flapped ineffectually at the wood, and Ambrose went to open it.

You locked me in here all night! I couldn't hear a thing!

"That was the point."

How would I have defended you from intruders?

"We were quite fine."

I thought I heard someone scream once.

"Definitely more than once."

Ambrose placed the snow-white box beneath the cloak.

"Watch this for me, will you? It's for Imelda."

I am a noble steed! Not a watchdog!

Ambrose patted the cloak, then headed for the door. He didn't trust himself to do more than glance at Imelda. But that single glimpse of her—soft and wild at once—felt like he'd lifted a corner of his future, and he wanted to run headlong toward it with his hand in hers.

As Ambrose raced down the staircase, he briefly wondered what message was waiting for him. But the thought fled his mind the moment he reached the bottom of the steps. There, standing in an extravagant fox stole and white gloves, was the witch herself.

"You look...well rested," she said knowingly.

Ambrose flushed. "I—"

"How was your little quest?"

"Good, my lady. We procured the potion you asked for."

"Find anything else?"

Ambrose thought of Imelda kissing him with such ferocity that he nearly lost his balance.

"Yes. We did."

"How nice for you both."

"We had a deal."

"And so we did! You wish for place and power, a position to rival your brothers, and I can give you just that. The moment you cross the bridge out of this winter town, you will forget all about this and find yourself on a road to a whole new adventure. I've laid it out splendidly! I found you a nice kingdom, plenty of good crops, a fair number of hardworking dragons, a river with not too many Lorelei inside so you don't have to keep an eye on drownings—"

"When we started on this quest, you said that...if we wanted... we could go back to Love's Keep. Er, I could go back. With Imelda."

"What an intriguing little turn!" the witch said happily. "Are you quite sure?"

"Yes."

The witch paused, and Ambrose didn't like that knowing glint in her eyes. "Have you asked her?"

Chapter 17

IMELDA

Imelda startled out of her dream at the sound of the closing door. Her eyes snapped open, a blush spreading across her face when she thought of last night. She'd never imagined she'd find such freedom in the small enclosure of Ambrose's arms. It was like escaping into a hidden kingdom, where the only time that mattered was the interval between kisses and the only dictate that held sway was whatever ratcheted the thrum of blood in her veins. It left her joyously untethered and feeling inexplicably *brave*.

Look at what she'd done for herself and no one else.

Look at how she'd reached forward instead of stepping back.

Look at how she'd emerged unscathed.

She wanted to prove to herself that she could do it again. Imelda grinned, reaching beside her in bed, only for her hands to be met with cold sheets.

"Ambrose?"

He dropped a box on me, mourned the horse cloak from the closet.

"A box?"

I don't like boxes.

"Where'd he go?"

Apparently, wherever it was did not require the presence of a horse. All he said was to watch the box because it was for you.

———

Imelda couldn't decide if she wished she'd never opened the box. Or if she was counting her blessings that she had. All she could do was stare at what lay within. Strange, she thought, that no matter how far away she got from home, a pair of shoes always put her in her place. It didn't even matter if they were enchanted to root her to the spot or yank her forward. They always had the same effect:

To remind her of control.

Ambrose's present was the loveliest pair of shackles she'd ever seen. Delicate glasswork slippers, with crystal roses and green ribbon vines that could be wrapped around one's ankle. A pair of translucent moth wings opened and closed at the heels, and the sound was like the chiming of chandelier pieces. Her aunt's words thudded in her skull.

"Trust me, child, he will try to control you, in the end. I know what you want, and the only way to get it is through power. Soon enough, you'll see. He'll just try to keep you down, and then what will you do? Better to look out for yourself, to love only *yourself."*

Tears stung at her eyes, and she knuckled them away. She was glad she'd seen this now, before she'd done something foolish. She'd been on the verge of asking that the witch give her the freedom not to go off on her own, but *join* him. To choose to give him her heart. To start over.

Footsteps pounded the stairs. She shoved the box into the closet, shutting the door despite the cloak's muffled protest. Imelda forced herself to stand, to pull herself together, even as something broke within her.

The door opened, and Ambrose crossed the threshold.

Chapter 18

AMBROSE

Ambrose hesitated at the threshold, trapped between the dictates of courtly etiquette, which bade him stand still and be courteous, and the fierce desire to gather her in his arms. Imelda was backlit by the sun, rendering her face inscrutable in the morning light.

"Imelda?"

She raised her head. Emboldened, he continued.

"The witch has returned for the potion and to give us our rewards."

"Rewards," Imelda echoed dully.

The words tumbled out of him. "Imelda, this past week, I thought perhaps we…we might start over. The witch even said she could bring us back to Love's Keep, and I thought, given all that's changed between us, we—"

"I'm not going back."

That tide of joy that had held him close this morning receded, and Ambrose felt the eternal winter chill of the town creeping into his bones. His ears felt hot, and he took a step forward. Imelda looked up at him. There was no softness in her golden eyes. Those lips he'd kissed over and over were still swollen, but pressed tight.

"I've only wanted freedom, Ambrose."

"What makes you think you wouldn't be free with me? You know me; I would never expect you to—"

"I know what I want," Imelda said coldly. "And it isn't you."

Ambrose felt something inside him shrinking fast. He had been so wrong. So *foolishly* wrong. He turned, a heavy weight settling on his chest.

"I'm sorry to have wasted your time."

"Wait!"

For a wild moment, his heart threatened to burst. He wanted to be proven wrong so badly, but the moment he turned, he caught something bristled and rough in his arms. The horse cloak shivered.

"You almost forgot that."

He fastened the cloak around his shoulders, forcing himself to look at her one last time. The moment he crossed the winter bridge, the witch's deal would go into effect. He would forget all about this quest and the year and a day he'd spent as her husband. He would have what he wanted: place, power, position.

But no Imelda.

And so, knowing that he would only hold this image in his heart for the next hour, Ambrose memorized his wife. He memorized the length of her lashes, the amber sheen of her eyes, and the feral twists of her hair. He memorized the slope of her neck and the way she rubbed the knuckle of her thumb when she was thinking. He memorized how she had laughed at him and drawn him outside himself. After all he'd memorized, Ambrose turned on his heel and walked out the door, determined to forget.

"I hope you find what you're looking for," Imelda said sadly.

Ambrose laughed, but it was a hollow thing. "The irony is that I already did."

Chapter 19

IMELDA

Imelda knew there was no freedom in love.

But there was no freedom in heartache either.

She sank to the floor, shaking violently. Barely more than a week had passed, and she finally had what she wanted. No one to answer to, no place to return to, nothing but the world stretched out before her.

The moment Ambrose left, Imelda shuddered. It was as if he'd taken all the warmth in the room with him. The armoire door was still open, revealing a corner of the snow-white box holding the crystal shoes. That one sight told her the witch queen was right... but if that were so, how come she didn't feel victorious? How come all she could see was the giddy smile on his face when he opened the door, the way he'd seemed to fight himself to stay still rather than go to her? How could that be the reaction of a man who would pin her down and drain her of freedom?

But the shoes didn't lie.

And all Imelda could do was congratulate herself for being proven right all along.

Chapter 20

AMBROSE

A mbrose knew there was no trust in love.

But there was no love in trusting that truth either.

Normally, he liked being right. But not this time.

The witch waited for him at the end of the staircase. There was an expectant gleam in her eye, and Ambrose wondered whether she knew all along that Imelda never planned to love him. Much less leave with him.

"All that you wish will come to pass," the witch said kindly.

Forgetting, thought Ambrose. That's all he wanted now. He didn't want to feel this chasm opening up inside him for a moment longer.

Hardly an hour ago, he was the happiest man in the world. He kept imagining different things…Imelda's face when she opened the present he'd given her. Her smile. Her kiss. Her hand in his.

"I just wish to forget all about this excursion."

"Then cross the bridge, my boy. But before you go, what about the stone potion?"

Ambrose pointed upstairs. "With her."

The witch smiled, casting her eyes upward. "Then it's time to pay her a visit."

Chapter 21

IMELDA

Y ou owe me a potion!"

Imelda looked up and saw the witch standing in the doorway of the room. She forced herself to stand, then pointed wordlessly at the stone potion, which sat on the windowsill behind her. The witch hummed to herself as she walked inside, plucked the bottle, and dropped it into her bright-pink purse.

"And what about me?" Imelda asked miserably. "What do I get?"

"The moment you leave this winter town, you will be forever unshackled. Your father will not expect you back in the palace. You will forget all about ever being the queen of Love's Keep and the past week—"

Imelda jerked her head up. "What?"

"Isn't that what you wanted? A new start? With my powers, you will wander the world, and I will give you a sturdy pair of seven-league boots, a purse full of enchanted roads, and a broad-brimmed hat because one should always limit exposure to the sun, or we age quite rapidly."

"But I don't want to forget."

Even if it had ended like this, she couldn't fathom losing

everything she'd seen, learned...*felt*...over the past year and a day and more. It struck her like a kind of death.

"You asked for freedom, child, but that's something I cannot grant you fully."

"But the deal—"

"The deal was for the sense of freedom, which you got without my assistance."

Sense of freedom? Imelda felt the sudden warmth of Ambrose's smile. That buoyant wave inside her heart. It *had* been freedom. But she couldn't trust it.

"Listen to me. You can wander the world and be beholden to no one, and still find yourself trapped." The witch shuddered. "That aunt of yours is no freer than a bird with clipped wings in a gold cage."

"No one controls her."

"Oh, perhaps it's not a person that pulls her strings...but it might as well be a tangible thing—blindness to love, lust for power, coiling envy, brewing suspicion. They will control you if you let them. But love? Love is a freedom. It is a land and a language that holds all, speaks to all—"

Imelda's eyes burned. "If it's such a freedom, then why did you take it from us all those months ago?"

The witch smiled. "You cannot take a thing like that. You could hide it, certainly, and there's power in the taking of memories. But if love is there, it will inevitably make itself known. Bit of an attention hog in that way, if you ask me. Tell me, did you find that something had made itself known between you?"

"It doesn't matter," Imelda snapped.

"No, of course not."

Imelda paused, exhaling.

"I won't love anyone who tries to trap me."

"Is that what he did?"

Imelda brought out the shoes and flung them down before the witch. The parcel opened of its own accord, the glass slippers glinting inside, the moth wings affixed to the heel stirring slightly.

"I saw the proof of it."

The witch raised an eyebrow. "I see a pair of shoes."

"Exactly! He knows how I feel about that. He knows how my own father used them to trap me and my sisters."

"Exactly. He does know."

Something in the way the witch said it made Imelda pause. She knelt to the ground, peering at the shoes. They looked nothing like the slippers her father had given to her and her sisters. They were too delicate. Not made for dancing to the point of breaking.

Imelda reached out, tracing the outline of the wings. At her touch, the slippers rose into the air, hovering at the height of her eyes. She startled backward, wonder zipping through her. A pair of flying slippers...the very thing she had once demanded, more out of jest than anything else. It was supposed to be impossible, and yet Ambrose had found them for her.

She rocked back on her heels.

Something nudged at the back of her thoughts.

Ambrose's voice in the moonlit copse of trees when she still held the statue's form.

"I never want to hold you down, Imelda."

Imelda shot straight to her feet.

"Oh."

"Mm-hmm." The witch sounded a bit bored.

Imelda ran to the window. Ambrose was halfway across the

bridge. Silvery snow whipped around his steps, quickly filling in the dips left behind by his boots.

"So what will you choose, Imelda? I can free you of any engagements, relationships, place, and property. Or…"

Imelda whispered, "Or I can free myself."

She thought of every time she'd felt hemmed in by the world of her father's kingdom, every moment she'd felt trapped in a marriage of obligation. She had thought love meant control, but a love of her own with no understanding of how its future might play out? *That* was a choice. A choice she'd never had until now. And she refused to lose it.

"The moment he crosses that bridge, he'll forget all of this. Even if you run, you won't make it."

"I can't run…but I can fly."

Chapter 22

AMBROSE

A mbrose looked at the end of the bridge.

Here, the glass sphere encasing the winter town was close enough to touch. Wind whipped up the snowflakes, and with each crunching step, his thoughts bent mercilessly around the image of Imelda's face.

One more step, and he wouldn't know it anymore.

He might see her years from now, and think only that she had strange eyes. He wouldn't remember anything of how they fluttered shut at a kiss or slanted at him in amusement and fury.

Shall we go trample something? That always makes me feel better.

"I thank you, but no."

Maybe Imelda will have a better idea.

"Imelda is no longer part of the picture."

Why?

"Because she doesn't want to be."

…Why?

"Because she flat out said so!"

I thought she was just looking for different shoes. She didn't like what you picked out. She made a funny sound.

Ambrose froze.

The shoes. She'd seen them. Maybe she didn't know what they were.

Or maybe he was a fool, and he should just keep going, forget all of this entirely. He took another step forward, the glass sphere inches from his face. All he had to do was walk through it. He squeezed his eyes shut, and her face swam before him: sly and fey-eyed. Days ago, he told himself that even if he lost her, at least he'd known her. At least he'd known what it had been like to fall in love with her.

So what was he doing?

Ambrose took a small step back, ready to pivot on his heel and race back to the inn, when a heavy boulder crashed into him, knocking him to the ground and screaming:

"STOP!"

Ambrose's head thudded painfully on the bridge. Snow blurred his vision. But he had enough presence of mind to know that boulders don't talk.

Imelda! the cloak shouted happily.

Ambrose's eyes flew open, and he propped himself on his elbows in time to see Imelda floating before him, her hair fanned out and her eyes shining. Something glinted at the ends of her dress, and Ambrose's jaw nearly fell open when he saw the pair of crystal shoes on her feet. For a long moment, they could do nothing but stare at one another. Eventually, he couldn't help himself...

He smiled.

Imelda glowered at him, an angry flush rising at the base of her throat when she noticed.

But that just made him smile more.

"You were going to go home without me. Which is extraordinarily rude."

Hope burst through his chest. He forced himself to a stand, drawing himself up.

Imelda said, "To me...you *are* home."

Imelda floated back to the ground, taking a step forward and reaching for his hand. Ambrose squeezed his eyes shut. He felt his ribs practically expanding just to hold in all that he felt.

"Are you sure? I need some kind of proof, Imelda, because I almost—"

Imelda grabbed him by the front of his shirt and kissed him.

Epilogue

Once upon a time, there was a king and queen—and a horse cloak who lived in the stables nearby—in a land called Love's Keep. Once, the king and queen had loved each other, but then they forgot, and then they remembered again. Much more than a year and a day has passed, but that does not stop them from remembering how to fall in love. Sometimes it takes coaxing and listening. Sometimes it takes laughter and tears. But the thread is there if you wish to lift it up to the light and follow it down whatever corridors of time it crosses through. For some, it is not worth the effort, and for others it is, and that is just the way of things.

The king and queen did not live happily, but *hopefully*, ever after. Which, in my opinion, is a far better compass by which to guide your life.

And that, my dears, is where their story ends.

About the Author

Roshani Chokshi is a *New York Times* bestselling author of young adult and middle grade fantasy, writing for Disney, Macmillan, and Audible. Her work has been nominated for the Locus and Nebula Awards and has frequently appeared on Best of the Year lists from Barnes & Noble, *Forbes*, *BuzzFeed*, and more. Her work includes the Star-Touched Queen duology, *The Gilded Wolves*, and *Aru Shah and the End of Time*, which was recently optioned for film by Paramount Pictures.